Hattie Brown

Catoninetales - A Domestic Epic

Hattie Brown

Catoninetales - A Domestic Epic

ISBN/EAN: 9783337242237

Printed in Europe, USA, Canada, Australia, Japan

Cover: Foto ©Andreas Hilbeck / pixelio.de

More available books at **www.hansebooks.com**

CATONINETALES

A DOMESTIC EPIC

BY HATTIE BROWN

A young lady of colour lately deceased at the age of

14

London:

LAWRENCE AND BULLEN,

169 NEW BOND STREET, W

1891

THE following brief Memoir, contributed over the signature of F. G. H. to the columns of the Mobile *Record*, at the date of Miss Brown's decease, gives us all that has been brought to light concerning the AUTHOR OF CATONINETALES.

HATTIE BROWN was born at Natches, Ga., where her parents were field-hands on the plantation of Mr. Jo. Fields. Little Hattie, named after one of the gentleman's daughters, was treated as a pet. Miss Fields, a first-rate musician, had also much taste for poetry, which she was in habit of reciting ; and Hattie, with the African faculty of imitation, so picked up the laws of measure as well as an insatiate ambition for original production. After the War the family came North, and earned a modest living in Boston, where at the period we edited the *Girls' Own*. Therein some of H. B.'s early verse had first appearance, submitted to us with a few ingenuous words stating the age of the writer,—11 years. The lines were distinctly too good for the age ; and we could not help instituting an inquiry that led to acquaintance with the family, poor but respectable, an acquaintance very soon ripening into a warm affection only interrupted by her untimely death.

The three dignities of poetry : the union of the true and the wonderful, the union of the beautiful and the wise, and the union of art and nature.

Triads of Catwg the Wise.

O for a quill from out a cat-bird's wing !

Young's Night Thoughts.

Quoth he then to the Drummer—Lay it on !   *Sterne.*

CATONINETALES

A DOMESTIC EPIC

COMPRISING A VERY TRUE AND DISMAL PATHETIC
NARRATION OF THE ENDS OF A MOST WORTHY CAT

KOK ROBYN

BEGINNING WITH HIS FIRST DEATH AND BURIAL
AND THE INQUEST THEREUPON

BY H. B.

For bonny sweet Robin is all my joy.   *As you like it.*

Robyn, jolly Robyn !   *Merry Wives, etc.*

Robyn ! good fellow !   *Midsummer Night's Dream.*

I thank you, Sir ! I shall be bold, I warrant you.   Have
you a stool there to be melancholy upon ?

> *Every man in his humour.*

B

What say you? Simon Catlin! *Romeo and Juliet.*

We have bespoke a CAT.

Anglo-Saxon CAT, Danish KAT, Swedish KATT, Old French, Irish, and Prussian CAT, Low German KATT, High German KATER and KATZE, Welsh CATH, Cornish KATH, Biscayan CATUA, Sclavonic KOT, American KAZ, KACH, Latin CATUS, Dic. Var. CATTE, &c.

His titles were

The Most Noble The Archduke Rumpelstiltzchen, Marquis McBum, Earl Tomlemagne, Baron Ratacide, Waowhler, and Skaratch.

There should be a court-mourning in Cat-Land; and if the Dragon wear a black ribbon round his neck, or a band of crape à la militaire round one of his fore-paws, it will be a becoming mark of respect.

Pancattantrums (Southey's Translation).

A Cat has nine lives and a woman nine cats' lives. *Old Proverb.*

And as the Katte hath nine lives, so also hath the Katte his taile nine vertebræ, whereof upon echone a several life dependeth.

Browne's Vulgar Errours.

What a monstrous taile our Cat has got. *Carey.*

Your Cat a mountain looks. *Shakspere.*

Silence awhile! Robin! take off this. *Id.* Mere cat-lap. *Anon.*

CATONINETALES
IN NINE FYTTES

The Funeral—The Fight—Love—Drowned—Margaret
—Hanged—Shot—Thanksgiving Day—Mystery.

And an end.

KOK ROBYN'S FUNERAL

His gite was golden gay with streakis blak. *Chaucer*.

WHO kill'd KOK ROBYN?   I
   I did, said Fanny;   VI
   I was set on by Danny: 3
   It was I kill'd Kok Robyn.

B 2

Who heard his groans?
    I did, said Union ;   4
    And growl'd in communion
While picking my bones.

Who saw him die ?
    I did, said Jack,   5
    As I lay on my back
Wide awake in one eye.

Who 's Funeral Boss?
    I am, said Nelly,   2
    Though my heart 's all a jelly,
A-quake at his loss.

Who 'll dig his grave?
    I will, said Father,
    Unless you would rather
Have some stranger knave.

Who 'll bear the pall?
    I will, said Timothy ;   7
    I 'll mind a limb o' thee :
So the chickens said all.

Who 'll be chief mourner?
    I, said O'Donoghue ;   8
    And no mother's son o' you'
'll do it forlorner.

Who 'll sing the psalm ?
    We will, said the Mice ;
    It will be real nice,
We re so blessedly calm,

And who 'll set the tune?
　We will, chirp'd the Birds :
　Don't ask us for words,
But we 'll manage a tune.

Who 'll preach the sermon ?
　I will, prosed a Rat ;
　I have it quite pat
From the text *Cats are vermin*.

――――――

Here ends our first story,
　One taile of Kok Robyn :
　Let us all stop our sobbin' !
We hope he 's in glory.

And now take note : as here-under wrote.

――――――

NOTE — 1 Robin's name, KOK ROBIN, which same did
our chief he-cat claim ; and VI delicit FAN, a she-setter,
a tan. 3 our chore-boy was, DAN.　Then UNION and
JACK, 4 tabby, 5 black, were our kittens, both born on a
midsummer morn of one mother, loved well by 2 Sister
NELL. 7 's a name that was flung at our rooster most
young ; and by 8 sure I mean our great ROOSTER DEAN,
of Irish descent. D, LEO, in went denoting a neighbour
as payment for labour in help of our plot.　Other notes
we need not.

――――――

Sir Kok's epitaph
Will be utter'd by LEO,　　　D
And his death-song.　Laus Deo !
　Let no one laugh !

THE EPITAPH

Here rests, his head and chest due-lapp'd in earth,
  A Katte to Fortune and to Fame unknown:
Much Science troubled not his kitly berth;
  Sad Poesy now makes his taile her own.

Now must we diverge to a right tuneful

DIRGE.

Dark Melancholy! mark!
Let never dog bark,
But loving cats hark
  And echo our moan!
Though myself but a dog,
Yet I feel that no clog
To my sorrows, which jog
  On in unison
With the mourners around,
Who me worthy found
With not too dogged sound
  T' accompany them
In these first obsequies
Of the friend that here lies
And to me did devise
  His fit requiem.
So I Leo, allow'd
A cat's name, here avow'd,
Of which Popes are proud
  In their haught catalog',
Find currage to lay
On this noble Cat's clay
What an advocate may
  Who is only a dog.

He was supple and brave,
As was proved by that knave
That brought him to his grave :
   I anticipate here :
But the words may remain,
For he has to be slain
Again, and again
   Till nine lives disappear.

He was striped like a pumpkin,
Had shoulders and rump thin,
And well could a jump win
   With any a-foot ;
Sleek was he and dainty ;
Steals, so, and why mayn't he ?
If not quite a saint, he
   Ain't less of a brute.

So to speak of him present :
The thought is unpleasant
Of him all decessant
   If not all deceased :
Though I 'd say to his face
That not one of his race
Has less call for the grace
   Of dog poet or priest.

For his gifts, they were great ;
What he stole, that he ate ;
For his faults, who shall state
   Any ill of the Dead ?
O, might I be likewise !

Pour, tears! from all eyes;
And the kind Destinies
Heave a stone at his head!

Sic transit Catus Mundi,
Translated Sunday.
And exit Leo.
What recks it me?
Oh!
Though this first fytte be ended,
Thereto is appended
SIR KOK's pedigree:
(Sacrificium laudis)
Which now sent abroad is
As written by me

H.B.

THE PEDIGREE

The cat-log of him. *Shakspere.*

His hatchment hangs "on the outer wall"
For every one to see;
And fit is it the world should know
Kok Robyn's pedigree.
Listen, dear lords and ladies all!
Lend willing ears to me!

He was a Catte of lineage high,
Which well-writ scrolls remark:
Of very ancient ancestry,
THE TWO CATS IN THE ARK:
A fact that's so remarkable,
I could not keep it dark.

'Mong his forbears was Fiddler Kat,
    When Kow o'erleap'd the Moon;
And the Cat that Mother Hubbard's Dog
    Was feeding with a spoon;
And on maternal side that Puss
    In Boots like a dragoon,

Carabbas hight.   Even royal blood
    He claim'd in line from him
Who, housed with a belovèd witch,
    One night went up the chim-
Ney, crying I am King o' the Cats!
    The taile is true, though Grimm.

In modern times one forerunner
    Was well-sung Gilbert Katte
Who Philip Sparowe slew, rehearsed
    By his own laureat.   (*Skelton*)
Tho' Cornish cats such tailes deny,
    Tailes may be long for that.

Still later, in the ways of trade,
    'Mong his grandsires came down
The Patron of Dick Whittington,
    Who brought him such renown
He purseveres at top o' 'Change
    In Troynovant's great town.

What child but oftentimes has read
    Of Goody Two-Shoes' friends?
The chief her Cat, a Cat of birth,
    Though here she condescends:

She knows that humble maiden's worth,
   And so her countenance lends.

See in heraldic books how high
   The House of CAT is placed !
The English Lion without spot,   *C.A.* 1
   The Scottish ne'er disgraced.   *C.A.* 2
What knight could bear a prouder crest
   Than Wild-Cat from the waist ?   *C.A.* 3

Or look again to elder lore !
   When Thor in Giant-Land
Put forth his godship in its power,
   Which nought else could withstand,
There was the Cat of Destiny
   To make him weak of hand.   *C.A.* 4

The greatest goddess Cybele,
   By Cats her coach is led ;   *C.A.* 5
And look where, following Bacchus' car,
   The wild-limb'd Mœnads spread,
And Fawns with Tigers dance to the tune
   In old Silenus' head.   *C.A.* 6

C.A. (*Caudal Appendage*) 1 2 Whether the Shield of England first
contained Lions or Libbards (leopards) has been the subject of many
serious inquiries. In the year 1235 Ferdinand, Emperor of the West,
gave Henry III three leopards for his coat.   *Casson's Heraldry.*
   In the Roll of Caerlaverock the banner of Edward I has 3 leopards.
   Lions in England's coat, says *Shakspere.*
   Leopards on thy shield, says *Walter Scott.*

C.A. 3 The Catesby crest : arms 3 cates or gingerbread cats.
C.A. 4 The Iceland Cat he could not thaw.   *Old Rune.*
C.A. 5 The Scandinavian goddess Freya also has her cat-charioteers.
   C.A. 6 Silenus swang this way and that.   *Wordsworth.*

And when that loose Saturnian crew
   The Titans did displace,   (*Ovid*)
And scamper'd the jovial Gods like beasts,
   Sol's Sister took Cat-grace
And swore she would die an old maid or
   A Cat: so made her race.

An old sky-myth : when storms invade
   The Moon-ruled realm of Night,
Diana, huntress chased and fair,   (*Jonson*)
   Appears to flee ; but light
Returns to chase the grey mouse clouds
   With re-Olympian might.   *C.A.* 7

Wise Egypt held Cats half divine,
   Their place to guard the Soul   *C.A.* 8
In royal tombs ; no people yet
   Have Cats consider'd foul,
Though rude art quite mistakingly
   Made Pallas' Cat an owl.

The goddess hight of Liberty,
   In her most high attaint   (*Livy*)
In haughty Rome, held at her feet.
   A Cat without complaint,
Imaging order'd liberty,
   True freedom, with restraint.

C.A. 7 " The Cat-Moon eats the grey mice of the Night." *Pan Cat-tantrums, Book* I, *chap.* 13. Pan-criti (cretur), the Hindu Goddess of Nature, drives a car drawn by countless myriads of Cats.

    C.A. 8 Ælurus was a Cat-headed God.

I pass, lest some deem me profane,
   The Cat of Judah's Tribe,
Saint Mark's too; but the Nemæan mark,
   To whom we must ascribe
This fame, Alcides claim'd his skin
   The gods themselves to bribe.

Sage Æsop fables to us how
   A Cat, which loved a man,
Became a woman for his sake
   And————but (the story ran)
A mouse disturb'd their wedded bliss,
   Before the bliss began.

Or take the story t'other way,
   Of the woman Cattish turn'd,
Saved only when her head was off,
   Her taile extremely burn'd!
There really is a power of things
   That might from Cats be learn'd.

Of Una and her faithful friend
   I may not dare to speak:
The maiden Truth so pure and bold,
   And Strength so maiden meek:
To retail Spenser, seems to me,
   Should task the soul of Cheke.

And other poems leonine,
   Too many much to quote,
Traverse the Nubia of my thought,—
   And most are known by rote:

My chiefest care has been to show
 There have been Cats of note.

Yet memories, meandering home,
 One saintlike Cat behold.
Whom Gregory (Nazianzen styled)
 To his great heart did fold,
A nimble Cat upon his knees
 To see the nimb of gold.

What families of history,
 Vouch'd histoiy, not myth,
And men of might in arts, and arms
 Of most heroic pith,
The name of Cat made honourable,
 If not so common as Smith ;

The Catos, Catius, Catiline,
 Catullus, widely famed
For song ; also Leonidas ; (*S. Catuldus too*)
 For race of Cat are claim'd :
Beside some dozen Popes,—of some
 Cats need not be ashamed.

That subtil Cat of Medici ;
 And Russia's lustiest dame ;
And Shakspere's Queen, may be divorced
 But not divorced from Fame ;
With Kate, the wild Kate of his love
 Petruchio cared to tame.

And Caterina Camoens,
 The Portingals' sweet flower,

Ay! sweet as Arqua's laurel bloom
    That Petrarch had for dower;
St. Catherine of the Wheel, pourtray'd
    By Raffaele's gracious power.

So Catherine-wheels, or cat-on-wheels,
    As pyrotechnics know:
July, or say November nights,
    They make a pretty show,
With boys and belles and squibs and shells
    And rockets all of a row.

Fireworks, flowers also named from Cats!
    The radiant Lion's-Teeth,
French *Dents-de-Lion ;* Lion's-Foot,
    Growing moist woods beneath,
Curing the snake's bite; Lion's Tail
    With many purpled wreath;

Cat-Tail (chair-bottoming); and mint
    (Cat-nep) by Cats esteem'd;
The garden darling, Lion's-Heart;
    The Lily, Leopard-schemed;
The particolour'd Tiger-Flower,
    The flower that Juno dream'd.

How numerous the Cat-Family!
    What names of ancient note!
How long the list when Noah discharged
    His Mesopotamian boat!
I wonder if the little Noahs
    Had all their names by rote.

The tawny monarch, golden-maned ;
    Tiger with tabbied skin
(Whence tabard); Panther, Eyra, Ounce ;
    Leopard, so lithe and thin ;
Rimau-dahan, and Catamount :   *C.A.* 9
    These but the list begin.

The Serval ; and the Chati, else
    The Chetah, fleet in chase ;
The Javan Marquay ; Caracal
    (Imperial Rome's disgrace) ;
The gaiter'd Lynx ; the Western world
    Has links of the same race.   *C.A.* 10

The real American Wild Cat ;
    The long-tail'd Ocelot ;
The Puma, Lion of the West ;
    The Jaguar,—for no spot
He 'd change with any pard alive,
    However streak'd his lot ;

The Chilian Colocolo ;—Back
    At the old East once more,—
The sandy Chaus o' Nile ; and look
    To Thebes, where dwelt of yore
Our Rob's immediate ancestors,.
    Now cemented o'er.   *C.A.* 11

C.A. 9 Rimau-dahan is the Sumatran tree-tiger. *C.A.* 10 Caligata is gaitered. The American wild cat according to Audubon is a lynx.

C.A. 11 Felis maniculata, the progenitor of our domestic cats, their mummies still remaining. See also their monuments at Thebes.

For pole "cats," skunks, and such small deer,
  Though, own we must, allied
And Aristotle-class'd as Cats,
  But on the sinister side,—
Feline Fitzclarensioux,—in such
  No Family Cat takes pride.

Rank,—yes! but not as CATS: the Greek
  Might be a martinet;
Mustepha Weasel, not a Cat,   (*Mustela?*)
  He on his ottoman set.
Faugh! fie! foumarts! what sense in that?
  I smell that gaily yet.   *C.A.* 12

Of all this tribe, this family,
  This gens, this powerful clan,
Their blood from many so noble source
  Through our Kok Robyn ran,
As run the rivers to the sea;
  No proudest Catalan   *C.A.* 13

Had bluer blood; and in his shell
  Of tortoise, one to vaunt,
He show'd grand as that Tortoise is
  That bears the Elephant
That bears the World. Hyperbolic?
  Be more exact I can't.

C.A. 12. The MS. here was doubtful. She might have written galè
(Greek for weasel); but very possibly used gaily (N. C. English) like
the French *joliment*, as just a strong expression.

  C.A. 13 The Tortoise-shell Cat is Spanish.

The tortoise hides (think not I mean
   The Hindu) I prefer
To black or white, or black and white,
   Or even the tabby fur:
A tortoise-shell Tom-Cat, they say,
   Is rare. Or say it were.

And such a tortoise-shell! No comb
   No coxcomb brought his bride
In variegated vanity
   Our well-comb'd Kok outvied:
No limner hand might paint that skin.
   And yet Kok Robyn dyed.

R.I.P.

Requiescat in pace!
English'd, Let him lie still!
Or, His cat-bones be aisy!
That 's pat,
By CATEQUIL.

NOTE. Reader! don't wonder at the oath I use:
Catequil is Peru's God of Thunder.
What could be more appropriate?
Kok Robyn is consecrate to Thor.

Cat-god, Purrsepolis.

C

NOTE BY THE EDITOR

The pedigreeable portion of the fore-going fytte appears
to have been borrowed from or at least suggested by an
old poem of the sixteenth century, by Lydius Cattus, put
afterwards into Dutch by one Jacob Cat, Cats, Catts, or
Catz, for the spelling cat-like is various. The FIGHT to
come follows the account of an affair with the Catti, after
the *Commentaries* of Cæsar, as translated by the French
historian, Catrow ; and is in some measure an imitation
of the *Galeomnomachia* of Theo. Prodonius.

From an ancient monument in
Pussé Church, Gironde.

THE FIGHT WITH THE DOG

By biting and scratching dogs and cats come together.   *Proverb.*

WHEN we got home from his funeral
  Kok Robyn came from the door:
Quoth he—I know I have lost a life,
  But my quoter says 8 lives more;
So, rubbing his ears against our legs,
  Went purring our steps before.

And now would you learn how Kok Robyn
  Again hath lost his life,
It was all along of his hob-nobbin'
  With a lady not his wife.
Love like Atropos' scissors can shear:
  Though my verse requires a knife.

This Lady Katte was a nigh neighbour,
  A Bywater by name;
Wherefore it happen'd that by water
  Our Kat his end became.
As well this end did him become:
  May my taile prove the same!

C 2

Kok Robyn, I'll own, had a character
  For wandering out o' nights,
Whereat no doubt, if some were glad,
  Some might not like such flights.
But who can stand in the window way
  Of an honest Kat's delights?

That ugliest Dog of Smith's you know,
  Half bloodhound and half bull:
He'd watch'd to see sweet Robyn go,
  And he promised him to pull.
O the ways of this unkinder dog
  Are verily sorrowfull.

Kok Robyn climbs to the top of the fence,
  In the smile of the honey moon;
Amuses his love with his mews and miaouls,
  Nor thinks to be maul'd so soon.
'Twas sweet to listen, his pleasant voice
  Discoursing to such a tune.

Very lightly down he alighted thence,
  But ere he could touch the ground,
Between a brace of wide-gaping jaws
  He met with a toothsome wound.
Never he dream'd that a dog of choice
  Would be prowling there around.

Yet brave as a lion our darling turn'd
  A spirit inform'd his paws,
His catly heart within him burn'd,
  In the foe he flung his claws;

A spit between the bark and the would,
  And then ───── terrific pause.

And away and away over fence and wall
  He flew, and the blacksmith after,
With many a stumble and many a fall,
  And a roar that was not of laughter.
Night heard the howl and the caterwaul
  And the sky-roof shook, each rafter.

And over the fields to the river-side
  The Dog and the dogg'd Cat sped,
All hidden in wounds too wide to hide,
  As each hied o'er the other's head.
And the smith the death of a dog has died.
  Then Kok Robyn fell down dead.

We found them so on the morrow morn,
  A sorrowful sight to see ;
And our feelings all were quite forlorn
  Through feline sympathy.
For the dog we cared not so much as Adàm,
  Had he died by the Apple Tree.

Our will was wild to bury our Dead
  Under an apple tree ;
But among the " greenings " we 'd a fear
  A " cats-head " sort to see ;
And what if every apple s'talk
  Kok Robyn's taile should be !

By certain of us it had been well held
  Where the streaked punkins grow

To bury his bones, and Nelly implored
    Indeed that it should be so :
But then to see punkins tortoise-shell'd
    And fiddle-strings inside.   No !

So we back'd him out across the road
    O'er the marshes with never a halt,
Not minding the trouble of such a load,
    For we loved him to a fault ;
Shyly and sadly we laid him out
    With an elegant sum o' salt.

And very much like a wail it was
    That rent the mouth o' the sack,
As Rob pass'd down to his ocean doom
    And the sea-nymphs stroked his back.
Seem'd that the heaven was only glass,
    And the world had gone to wrack.

My rhymes are wanting poetic guile :
    Could I rhyme like my master Poe,
It mightn't you rile to place your pile
    On the tears I would bid to flow.
A dead taile, hardly worth wagging-while
    I sprinkle damp words on now.

MORAL :—Would Cat and Dog agree,
    As Watts his name once tried,
As it is their nature too,—says he.
    Our Cat and Dog first died.
Yet the lion lies down with the lamb,
    When the lamb-chops are inside.

Kok Robyn's name is on the wind,
His body has gone to sea :
He has yet seven other lives of a mind
To lengthen his memory,
Beyond this taile just left behind
For the Mews of History.

LOVE

With cat-like watch. *As you like it.*
Care will kill a cat. *Wither.*

DAN CUPID, 'tis well known,
Both men and cats doth own :
No creature left alone
By him. Here make I moan
Of wrong that he hath done
My Catte, my Robyn dear,
My favourite, my fere,
My Catte withouten peer.
Would Cerberus he were here!

My Robyn !—Every dame
Who cattish blood could claim
Held Robyn well in mind ;
As favourably inclined

Cat damosels were also.
Many a pleasant throe
He flung in Misses' hearts,
So perfect were his parts,
So lovely eke his looks,
Like cats in gospel books ;   (*Roydon*)
And his demeanour staid,
That never properest maid
Need be of him affray'd,
So debonair and meek.
He had too little cheek.
And his best coat so sleek !
He never miss'd a week,
Nay ! never miss'd a day,
To brush the dust away.
His sleekness took no hurt,
For the least speck of dirt
He wiped off with his tongue.
His whiskers too were long,
Becoming one so young ;
His eyen were so clear ;
And on each pretty ear
There was a tip of black,
The same along his back ;
And his fine mottled sides
Were beauteous as hides
Of tortoises, or shells
Which whosoever dwells
By the sea-shore is apt
To value.   When he lapp'd
His cream you did perceive
'Twixt jaws a foe could reive

His tongue's rich coral red,
Fit tongue of so rare head !
And when he flung his taile
As thresher throws his flail,
You felt he could not fail
In fight with other male.
O Catte delightful ! hail
Even to that form so pale,
Dim and untortoiseshell'd,
In visions oft beheld !
My grief is partly quell'd
By history of his fate,
The taile I here relate.

Be sure that highest dames
At Robyn took their aims :
A hope no mother shames.
Each sought to fix for life
Her daughter as a wife ;
And all the neighbourhood
And to a distance would
Echone have wed her child
To him, the Unbeguiled.
The girls, they all were wild
To win the love of him.
Many bright eyes grew dim
Weeping for him away ;
Many a maid would stray
From the parental home,
And anywhither roam
In vain hope to surprize
One glance of his dear eyes.

And if by chance they met
The welcome he would get
From virgin looks abash'd
All daring hope had dash'd
Of other loving swains.
I tell not of the pains
Mothers and daughters took
That he might only look
With favour on love-chains:
Labour that had no gains,
For no chains did he brook.

A lusty bachelor
Was he that time; and for
The love of cats most fair
And tender had no care,
No more than a cold frog.
His heart was yet a Log,   (*Æsop*)
Nor apt his neck to crane
After sly Beauties fain
To love him and complain
Not being loved again.
He better liked a sweet
Nice juicy bit of meat,
Of mutton, beef, or pork,
Which he took on a fork
Full seemèly, nor raught. (*Chaucer*)
Delicate mice he caught
Were daintier, he thought,
Than school-girl cats, howe'er
Fine-eyed or fine of hair;
And many such there were.

No Chartreuse pious grey,
No lop-ear of Malay, *
Or Madagascar Miss
With twisted taile, to bliss
Of Hymen could twist him ;
White Persian hope grew dim,
Silky Angora's slim,
As certain both to fail
As Manx Maid scant of taile.
No wooing might avail
With this unfeeling male,
He wanted no sweethearts :
The gizzards and tit-parts
Of chickens he prefer'd,
Or a plump youngling bird,
Or toothsome tender rabbit,
Had he the luck to grab it.
Even tailes of rats or mice
Were to his taste more nice
And held of more account
Than all that love-amount.
Love-tailes were so absurd :
For he if young had heard

---

* NOTE by the Editor. The Chinese Cat has long pendant
ears, rabbit-like. The Malayan Cats and those also of the Isle
of Madagascar are distinguished by their tails being curiously
twisted or knotted. Miss Brown's natural history is generally
most remarkably correct ; in the present instance however she
has, it would appear, confounded the peculiar characteristics of
the Chinese with those of the Malayan variety. She will not
often be caught tripping, even in her liveliest moods.

A scrape of wisdom's saw
From his old grandam; Law!
She used to say: my dear!
You keep from misses clear!
Quite time enough to wed
When I am gravely dead.
Certes she did not care
To have her easy chair
Invaded by a wife;
And she mislikèd strife,
And would not be too free
With Mrs. R.—not she,
For worlds.   I lose my taile.

One night they did prevail
On Rob.   It was a time
Of early frosts.   The rime
Just whiten'd like a cake
The very first day-break,
But had not strength to hold.
The evenings were that cold
That schemers young or old
Might find excuse to sleep
Before the fire, or keep
Alive with moving tailes.
Well, one of these females,
An old cat-dame, prevails
On Robyn to attend,
And Bob White too, a friend,
Their dozings to partake.
Or join them in a wake,
A soirée musicale,

Anglicè Cattes' night squall.
Venìt, vidìt, vicìt!
The English, Ma'am! of it
Is first—he came and sat ;
Second—he saw his Catte ;
And third—what hap'd of that.
Such poor Cæsarean wit!

The Catte he sat beside
Was comely and her hide
A pleasant kind of black. (*C.A.* 15)
Well could she arch her back,
And ripply as a river
Her slender taile would quiver
When sadder tailes oppress'd
Her gentleness of breast.
But if she were but pleased,
She musically eased
Her bosom with a purr,
Persistent as a burr
Upon a length of fur.
Black was she, as I said,
But when the sunshine play'd
Upon her velvet skin,
Outsiders, taken in,
Took her for tabby,——lo!
Gold stripes appear'd in row

C.A. 15 "Black but comely" is, I am told, the true rendering of
the text of Solomon ; but in our American Bible (published in 1842
by the Messrs. Lippincott of Philadelphia) which my dear Miss
Fields gave me when we came North, I find it corrected to "dark
but beautiful."

Along her sides ; taile, head,
Were fairly zebraèd,
And radiant grew each hair.
For grace she might compare
With best She in a year
You 'd find.   Her eyen clear.
Right proper she, I ween,
To be our Katt-King's Queen,
Majestic although slim,
A consort worthy him.
So leaping at her side
His heart chose her for bride.

And she mew'd up, unwoo'd
Before, would what she could,
A virgin young and raw :
She lifted up his paw
And lick'd it, as to say
" I 'm yours, to love, to obey,
And honour,—or of that
All may become a Catte."
I am not rude to tell
Young lovers' transports.   Well !
She loved and troth did plight.

And he loved her.   Next night
He for his Lady's sake,
His love-thirst too to slake,
Bethought him he would take
His presents to her bower :
No matter what.   The hour
Was right for a cat-call.

He nears the house——A squall,
A spit, and over the wall
A skurry! What is she
Those revels leads? Ah me!
What is it that he sees?
That Most Adored of Shes
Coquetting: on his knees
A male Catt, his friend White.
Dark Fate! how fell thy spite.
Home went he back that night,
Thought of his yester-kiss,
Thought of his now lost bliss,
Thought all the world a miss,
Saw all her falsehood through,
Foresaw young piebalds too,
Forgave her, knew his part
Was play'd.
        Then broke his heart.

GLOSSARY

AND TABLE OF EXPLANATIONS

for the occasions of the unlearned and undictionaried :
(authorities varied.)

CATALEPSY — When the cat-ropes are over tight in the fit. Heart-action however may continue.

CATAPASM — *v.a.* To dust : *e.g.* a boy's jacket. Found efficacious in cases of feint.

CATAPLASM — Mustard or other provocative or preventive according to the mode of application. An epithem.

CATSUP — Favourite drink of Cats ; made of mushrooms.

CATONIC — The old Roman hari-kari.

CATAPULT — An engine of peculiar cataballative quality.
                                    P. Cox *Headlong Haul.*

CATADUPE — When a Cat is fooled by being flung into the river, as in our second fytte.

CATAMARAN — A flat-bottom'd Cat's boat for fishing.

CATANDROMOUS — Going seaward, returning salmon-like.

CATABASIONED — *v.p.* To be preserved, in sea-catacombs pickled, as a relic.

CATALYSED — Thawed, resolved into adieu. *Shakspere.*

CATAGMATIC — With a view to bone-mending.

DROWNED

Thrice the brinded cat hath mew'd. *Shak pere.*
Never was cat drowned that could see the shore. *Proverb.*

THE CUCKOO-CLOCK proclaims our supper-time :
   Not often at this hour doth Robyn leave.
Surely he must have heard that cheery chime !
   Where is he wandering this wintry eve?

Stare not at me apostrophizing so
   Our dear dead Robyn of whom late I spoke
As broken-hearted ! He is dead, I know ;
   But hearts are patchwork, to be mended broke.

Yes ! he was dead. The morrow of that day,
   More truly of that sad eventful night,
Found was he, stark and stiff ; my sister May
   Ran to me horrent-hair'd in tremulous fright.

'Twas catalepsy, said they,—a mistake !
   The cataleptic is devoid of sense :
Dead or alive his sensitive heart would ache.
   And some brute said, may be it 's all pretence.

D

We catapasm'd him,—tried sorts of salts,—
    Hot irons,—brimstone baths,—of no avail :
We might as well have taught the Cat to waltz
    Steeping in catechu his stiffen'd taile.

We wrapp'd him in a potent cataplasm :
    It took the skin clean off his stomach fair,
But gave him no relief. One wrinkling spasm,
    And he was off again, like a singed hair.

At length he oped his melancholy eyes,
    One little crack in the iris of our hope ;
Sigh'd, wink'd and sneezed, so wink'd again and sigh'd
    As taking side with life : as one the rope

Has fail'd to finish on the gallows tree.
    Such similes be hang'd ! We brought him to ;
But knew three lives were gone, yes ! surely three,
    A third of his nine tailes, if tailes be true.

And since that death he was an alter'd Cat :
    Took much to drink, catsup ; stay'd out o' nights,
In spirit haunting her. Blame not for that !
    He only did according to his lights.

Heart-broken quite, his little bark a wreck,
    Grown cynical, he reck'd not where he sail'd :
Some times his fancy paced hope's frailest deck,
    Others his fancy's tether was curtail'd.

Who, who shall medicine a mind diseased ?
    Throw physic to the dogs ! Why catechise ?

We gave him sedatives,—he only sneezed ;
  Gave morphia,—and we slept not for his cries.

For in his dreams he saw that heartless thing
  That slew him ; then did he unsheathe his claws,
His taile stood up on end, and he would fling
  His wild legs out without a thought of pause.

And day and night he 'd wander, sighing sore
  For that so beauteous and most faithless sake.
Dead was he, could we but have said no more :
  Alive, a set of bare bones with an ache.

And he perhaps had slain himself again :
  Once, twice, upon the sharp sword of his woe
Had harikaried, but for this refrain—
  He might miscarry throwing six, you know.

No laws of honour or the best Japan
  Prescribe continuous Catonics, so he
Dead might survive, to endure for yet a span
  The hopeless lover's love-lorn agony.

From the poetic vision nought is hid :
  This asking why he comes not is a sham ;
I knew while looking at the tea-pot lid
  He could not come, no more than a dead clam.

The eyes of sense were on the coffee-grounds ;
  My spirit track'd him as he slowly pass'd
Along a field-side, then with sudden bounds
  Beheld him over the fences, till at last

D 2

I watch'd him by the river, glancing down
   Sadly upon the tide, high tied with frost;
I knew the ice was thin, to him unknown;
   I knew if he should try it he 'd be lost.

I saw him gaze (O that disconsolate gaze !)
   Upon the desolate waste; then in a trice
On his four legs his heavy body raise
   And catapult-like heave it on the ice.

A cataract supervened. I thought his eyes
   Must suffer from the cataract or the scratch;
I thought of his weak health,—'twas so unwise
   To marshal strength a mere catarrh to catch.

When last we cataduped him he came back!
   Is he catandromous now? To let him through
The ice was thin enough, but not to crack
   From underneath. What will poor Robyn do?

O my, Kok Robyn! why is Death thy foe?
   Where art thou now? my Cat, my gracious!
Under the grim flood of Cocytus slow   (*Spenser*)
   Thy dwelling is in Erebus' black house.

There the young imps of Night, first wife of Death,
   Play "cat" with thee, and find their fell delight
Striking thee up, seeing thee out of breath
   And falling headlong like a tail-less kite.

Reflection brings thee to thy briny grave,
   Dump'd on a heap of grimy oyster-shells,

Where o'er thy corse funereal sea-weeds wave,
   And nasty sea-nymphs hourly ring thy knells.

A damp ghost in a catamaran he roams
   A-fishing through the forests of the sea,
His catabasion'd bones in the catacombs
   With piscid skeletons of high degree.

Or if not yet quite thoroughly catalysed,
   Can he get flesh on clams? O Cat alive!
Albeit some squalid cat-fish (*squalus*) so apprised
   May hospitably for thy health contrive.

Mayhap some blue-hair'd Nereid pick'd him up,
   Catagmatic: on her cold knees he stays,
Learning on sailor sausage how to sup,
   And sea-cow's milk. I hate their fishy ways.

Perchance some whale like Jonah gobbled him:
   Will he return like Jonah? Who shall say?
Five-lived he roves in those recesses dim,
   Praying for him who took him for a prey.

If the same whale as Jonah's, may it please
   The Prophet, might such be his horrorscope!
That whale, so is it writ in Portuguese, (*Southey*)
   Doubled as Jonah's bark the Cape Good-Hope.

I can not think him lost to me: perhaps
   Some cataclysm may lend a helping hand,
Picking our darling's bones from marine laps,
   Throwing him up upon his native land.

Time has to show.   But, Hattie! while your gaze
    Intreats the Future for his welcome ghost,
The tea is cooling.   And her father says—
    The Cat be d———d (that's drown'd)—
                                    Pass me the toast!

For hard words turn back to Glossary at page 32.

MARGARET

In Sanscrit Margaras or Margery, Cat-liking.

THE NEXT TIME our Kok Robyn died,
    It fell upon this wise,—
A foolish thing, but children's deeds,
    They need not much surprize :
The biggest baby may not know
    The reason of its sighs.
Men are but children of a larger growth,
And groaning an accomplishment of both.

A gentle girl was Margaret,   *(Nell's sister)*
    Yet sturdy therewithal :
No lass was nimbler on her pegs,
    And, good in Spring or Fall,
She liked fair weather courtesies
    And didn't mind a squall.
Upon our back-door step this happy child
Sat with a lunch in hand and eating smiled.

Our rare red Margaret ! her cheeks
    Like tips o' the daisy-flower,

Our Pearl of girls, with divers gifts
  Of loveliness and power:
Her smiles were like a morn of May,
  Her tears an April shower,—
Of May and April in those steady climes
Where months return at their expected times.

It was the pleasant time of Spring,
  With Summer coming fast;
The frogs were all a-caroling,
  Old Winter gone aghast:
Though frogs sing well he better likes
  The song of a Nor-east blast.
De gustibus non est——I 'd rather hark
To a full bull-frog chorus, after dark.

A chunk of thickly-butter'd bread
  She held in either hand,
The butter under,—'tis a thing
  That children understand;
And our Kok Robyn went and came
  At the dear child's command,
Well pleased to share his lady's humble fare.
'Twas partly with that purpose he was there.

Now Meg, though not a miller's gir
  Nor Trulliber at all,
Did like her bread and butter and,
  When chanced so to befall,
A puff of jam. Her appetite
  Was certainly—not small.
She gave a solid magnum to the Cat;

But he Tom-like was not content with that.

And as he ate she would him chide,
　　With "Daddy! why is this? *C.A.* 16
You've been away so long of late
　　From me, a woeful miss.
For I did miss you, Robyn dear!"
　　Here she gave Rob a kiss.
"How wet you are, my love! and, dear! your skin
Tastes very salt: my sweet! where have you been?"

She spoke but truth: much had she grieved
　　For Robyn, lost of late,—
For she had loved him from his birth,
　　In his most kittenish state.
The fourth abduction of her dear
　　Had left her desolate.
She spoke as mothers do when their lost heirs
Come home escaped from drowning unawares,

Scolding to hide her pride of heart,
　　For she on him had spread
Love butter-like; he calmly lick'd
　　The butter from her bread.
"O Robyn! you are naughty, Sir!
　　Get off my lap?" she said,
And push'd him off; he coming to the ground
Chevied his barr'd tail for a moment round,

C.A. 16 In Sanscrit Dadhi-karnas, or Butter-ears, is the Cat with
the white or butter (cream) coloured ears which my Robyn had.
See the *Pancattantrums* again. The jackal is Dadhi-pucchas, or
Butter-tail.

Then stroll'd away, displeased, in scorn
    Of bread and mistress' wrath.
Near by the ash-barrel stood, in which
    He jump'd, and quickly hath
Pick'd out a fish-bone. Will he take
    Again a fishward path?
I can not tell you what kind 'twas of bone:
Perhaps the name to him was not unknown.

I said that he was Margaret's pet:
    In youth, even now not old,
She 'd bear him in her pinafore,
    Or wrap him from the cold
In her warm cloak: but little chance
    Of straying from that fold.
Yet he would stray, the Irish Scripture says
Skedaddle, scattering on many ways. *C.A.* 17

So pretty was it in that time
    To see the child-like Puss
Chasing his shadow and racing like
    Some little human cuss,
Frisking about so frolicsome.
    It was great fun to us,
The elder children, but to Margery
It was a play she never tired to see.

For him she 'd drag the ball of thread—
    'Twas mostly worsted, drew

C.A. 17 This in an old Irish Bible : I will smite the shepherd and
the sheep shall be "squdad ol." *Mark, chap.* 14, *ver.* 27, and
elsewhere.

For him an imitation mouse,
    Or made the kit leap through
Her guardian hands ; and many a trick
    The merry playmates knew.
He was her brother, lover, and her child ;
And he then young was also love-beguiled.

It was her wont to watch the birds :
    The thrush's scarlet throat
Pleased her, and of his namesake she
    Had learn'd the fate by rote,
Indeed by heart, and of Jane Wren
    To Robyn so devote :
So she unto her favourite gave the name
Of Kok Robyn, and this one is the same.

What ails him now? thinks Margaret.
    Upon the grass he lies.
What strange reflections doth he make?
    How opalesque his eyes !
And from his mouth projects a bone
    Which with forepaws he tries
To wrench away. Alas! the bone is stuck
Too fast. O woe for her poor Robyn's luck.

Her end of bread and butter dropt,
    One rush into the house,
A scream, a real Spring burst of tears,
    And then her head falls souse
Into her marveling mother's lap.
    No little cat-scared mouse
E'er faster ran than she from fear of Rob,

And scarce could speak for interpose of sob

That shook her.   But at last between
Her sobs came out one word :
"Rob," sob, then " Rob," then sob : in this
Same order they occurr'd.
'Twas quite a while ere any one
The true adventure heard.
Then we went out and found him lying there,
Dead, choked, with all his legs like telegraph
poles in the air.

Nothing is gain'd by sighs, my dear !
Musing to Meg I said.
Though you were twice as big, I fear,
The Cat were no less dead.
These things remain among the queer ;
And now it 's time for bed.
So I choked off the choked one's little mourner,
And happily swung my taile to Finis Corner.

HANGED

Hang me in a pudding-bag like a cat ! *Shakspere.*
As a cat likes mustard. *Proverb.*

O HANG THE CAT ! said Martin :
   But before it went that rough
We had suffer'd no end of trouble
   And given him rope enough.

We had spring chickens that summer,
   A very promising brood ;
And Robyn he went a-poaching
   Like any Robin would. (*Hood ?*)

Poach'd eggs we never had minded,
   But chickens black and tan,
Poach'd in the cook's own manor,
   And not in a frying-pan.

Three black, and two of a lovely brown,
   One speckled, and one all white :
And the nasty thief, he ate them raw ;
   ·   And the last was a favourite.

I have implored him, almost with tears,
  In a most intreating tone,
Assuring him when the chicks grew up
  He never should lose a bone.

I 've even been on my knees to him,
  Many a time and oft,
Proving how wise it would be to wait :
  But he never was that soft.

I pray'd him for love of his mistress dear
  To let those nurslings alone ;
But ever he turn'd a deafer ear,—
  He "liked them not full-grown."

Then we muster'd two or three deceased
  (Mustard, they said, would check
His appetite), and we tied the least
  Tight round the caitiff's neck.

We laugh'd at the grim grimace he made,
  O we all did laugh amain
As he tasted it first, but he muster'd hope
  And went for a lick again.

Why, the chick was just as yellow all o'er
  As if it wore down of gold ;
I felt how his poor mouth would be sore,
  And I hadn't the heart to scold.

He tugg'd at the string, it didn't break ;
  Then he lick'd the mustard off

And ate up his necklace all but the string
　　With never a sneeze or cough.

Nothing he cared : he the mustard lick'd
　　And he neither purr'd nor swore ;
But, the second drumstick nicely pick'd,
　　Went off and drumm'd for more.

And every season following that,
　　With seasoning or without,
He seem'd to savour his poultry more :
　　Our broods so came to nought.

So Cook and Martin a plot they laid
　　To bring Kok Rob to grief.
They borrow'd of Pa a ball of twine
　　To cure the chicken thief,

They gave him hinder quarters in
　　An elegant pudding-bag,
And tied his fore-paws up with tape,
　　And stopp'd his jaw with rag.

They drew the cord of the bag quite fair
　　One end of it held by each,
Not close,—with just enough of room
　　For a penitent's dying speech.

Draw tight ! said Martin, and the twine
　　He pull'd. The Cat was dumb.
'Twas Cook that yell'd : inside the cord
　　The Cook had poked her thumb.

And Robyn, he dropp'd into the bag,—
    They dared not view his corse.
And if he shamm'd, or if the Cook
    Was smitten with remorse,

Or of mere tender-heartedness,
    As cook'd hearts may be so,
She thus had kindly thrust her thumb,
    Intent to let him go,

Or if a miracle (who knows?)
    Had spared his sixthly breath,
Or if one of his four-left lives
    Was forfeited to Death,

Shall not be known until the end,
    When all nine lives are gone
    And he arises to reclaim
    His last vertebral bone.

The pudding-bag, Kok Robyn's shroud,
    Was missing from that day.
Was Robyn buried in it? or did
    He carry it away?

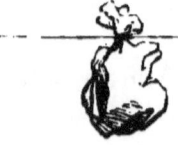

SHOT

Thrice to thine and thrice to mine and thrice again to make up nine.
Shakspere.

SWIFTLY our Indian Summer came and went :
   The crimson maple leaves were trampled down,
The yellow chestnuts in one storm had spent
   Their gold ; and now the woodside all was brown,
   Save for some hemlock standing in its gown
Of green perennial. Then there came a snap
   Of biting cold. That too had come and gone ;
And warmer days return'd, with pleasant hap
For the sun-loving things on kindly Nature's lap.

The birds, collecting for their southern flight,
   Drifted around our homestead. Fine times these
For Master Robyn,—who ere morning's light
   Clomb to the roosts upon the leafless trees
   And caught the helpless sleepers at his ease ;
Then to his larder, the top cellar-stair,
   Took them, a sight that might his mistress pleaso
Thought he. She waken'd, he would make repair
To show her of his prey and providential care.

E

But not content with plentiful supply,
    Brought daily to his board, of choicest food,
His greed, or wantonest fancy, would set by
    Home-sureties for chance forage in the wood,—
    In sooth a too inviting neighbourhood.
Here would he roam, still seeking newer game;
    And of his prowess proud as Robin Hood
Rejoiced him in the wild,—he scorn'd the tame.
Meseems that beasts and men are verily the same.

For also through this woodland often pass'd
    The idle fowler out for holiday.
Well, Robyn, fowling too, his quick eyes cast
    Upon a tree whereup a squirrel grey
    Was running, like a lightning run wrong way.
Good cheer! said Robyn, following up the tree.
    The fowler saw but Skug; ere one could say
Back, Robyn! he had fired; and Robyn he
Received the leaden fare sent as the squirrel's fee.

And like a lump of lead, so Robyn fell.
    A Cat-bird, close at hand, beheld his fall
And caught the accents of his passing yell,
    Forthwith repeating it with sudden call,
    So like unto a four-legg'd caterwaul
That all the birds were frighten'd at the sound;
    Till he, the many-voiced, address'd them all
In their own music, hastening them around
To note the Cat as trophy lying on the ground.

Bidding them to the great Cat's funeral games,
    And calling on them, each and every one,

With summons to them by their several names
  To attend. But willing answer he gat none,
  Perch'd on his bough, the dead Cat o'er, alone.
Only the hawk high hovering, skied and free,
  Shriek'd from his poise "the game is all my own."
And the half-waken'd owl, hid in his tree,
Repeated "all my own" and hooted out his glee.

The other birds,—the bobolink, the thrush,
  The oriole, the wren, the chickadee,
And every bird that singeth from a bush,
  Or skyward soars, or through the grass goes free,
  Gave answer, one and all, "What fools were we
To honour him with mourning who hath slain
  So many of us. Our worst foe was he.
Wherefore instead of sorrow let us strain
Our tuneful throats in thanks to the Caticide again."

Thus they exultingly. Meanwhile the Dead,
  Only cat-dead, crawl'd painfully away.
He could not die in peace so canopied
  With just reproach. All through that weary day
  He dragg'd him step by step; oft had to stay,
For pain; but reach'd at last our garden fence,
  Powerless to clamber o'er. There let him lay!
False grammar? Byron wrote so. What pretence
Have I to better him? You understand the sense.

Next morn was bright and sunny; he lay there
  (Lay there is right) all motionless, quite dead.
What wandering voice, or wind, or bird in the air,
  To the other side his hapless story said?

                                        F. 2

Said, sang, or scream'd in strophes doleful, dread :
Scarce heard when lo! upturning all the mould
    Of the garden plot, and resonant in the red
Glare of the morning, rose a hubbub bold,
A full funereal catch, madriggled, manifold.

For all the creatures which had cause to fear
    The lives of birds redeem'd by Robyn's death
Came swarming forth, with lamentations drear
    For him to whom they owed their lease of breath ;
    All things above the earth or underneath
Whom birds feed on came out to proffer grief,
    With ceremonial dues of dirge or wreath,
For the great Bird-Devourer. Forth from leaf
And bark and root they came, a number past belief.

The Caterpillars first, as next of kin,
    The sad procession headed. First of these
The Arctian Tiger fleet of foot and thin,   1
    Though seeming bulky in his coat of frieze,
    Bristly and tufted. Next, in their degrees,
The Leopards, Yellow Bears, and Ermines paced ;
           2   3   4
    And Salt-marsh Caterpillars who from seas   5
Unable to escape, by the tide out-raced,
Roll themselves up in balls, so are in safety placed.

These more or less were kinfolk. 'Mong the rest
    In the front rank with mighty Polypheme,   6
Was seen Ceratocampa's royal crest   7
    Of orange black-tipp'd horns that almost seem
    To hurl you high defiance,—one might deem

Some warrior donn'd such head-gear, natheless he
  Foe-ward is harmless as an infant's dream.
With them green-clad Cecropia.   All the three   8
Were giants.   Follow'd them a lowlier company.

The warted and scant-robed Liparians;   9
  The crested Sycamore with orange hood;   10
The thornless, downy, soft Egerians;   11
  The pale blue Communist, misunderstood;   12
  The Zebra, learneder than I who could   13
Those runes decipher written on his back;
  The Velled scarce distinguishable from wood;   14
The Loop-worm, archly bent upon his track,   15
As fear'd to march too fast, in dread of some attack.

The Skipper, noted for his cleanly house;   16
  The tufted, particolour'd Harlequin;   17
The tufted Owls, that on the maple browze;   18
  The slender Spindle-worms with hairless skin,   19
  Corn-witherers they; Tent-Habiters who spin   20
Their path from twig to twig, from leaf to leaf,
  Holding a clue for safe returning in
From foraging; the Cut-worm, greasy thief!   21
Whose greed to the gardener is so daily ground of
                                              grief.

The naked Hunchback with his sixteen legs,   22
  If legs which sometimes barely pass for feet;
The Apple-Attila, whose hundred eggs   23
  Lie in one patch till hatch'd by summer heat;
The Wood-Nymph and the Ruiner of Wheat, 24 25
  Venomous Maia, and Ephestion brown;   26 27
  The Borer of the Peach, who hath his seat   28

Within the bark; the Tussock, hickory-known; 29
And Dryocampa who sets stoutest oaks to groan. 30

The Parsley-worm in robe of apple-green   31
   Spotted with black and yellow alternate,
With orange-colour'd horns,—he came between
   The pale green Cabbage-Eater and the great 32
   Thorn-tail'd Potato-worm; the elm-tree's hate, 33
Horn-shoulder Sphynx and poplar Porcupine; 34 35
   The grape-destroying Hog, in native state;   36
The dog-tail'd Devastator of the Vine :—   37
Slowly they crept along, a long funereal line.

The bristly Hedgehog, brush-like closely shorn; 38
   The Fall Web-worm, of greenish yellow hue, 39
Black-dotted and black striped, who leaves forlorn
   Our autumn trees; the Luna, greenish blue; 40
   The Forest-Pest, black yellow lined, that thro' 41
Great woods devouring passes; Io spined;   42
   The Locust Cossus, the Sack-Bearer too; 43 44
Slowly, with lingering steps, came on behind   45
The Shrivel'd Hag, or Slug, so sluggish is her mind.

After these march'd a multitudinous crew :
   All shapes, all colours,—greyish white and red
And tawny yellow, black and green and blue,
   Orange, ash-grey and purple, striped, or spread
With various spots, some horned, some with head
Crested and body many legg'd and long :
   Fruit-spoilers, borers, spinners of the thread,
Six-eyed, and claw'd, with jaws and nippers strong :
A motley many-visaged life-destroying throng !

This monstrous swarm of Lepidopterous birth,
   Too numerous to recount, such hosts are here,
Came honouring the virtue and great worth
    Of Him the BIRD-SLAYER who year by year
    Had charter'd them to live unvex'd by fear,
To increase and multiply. Protector now
   Was none save men or boys who nought revere,
Who shoot poor birds at rest on some near bough,
Or rob their nests: such thefts O why does Law
                      allow?

The Lepidoptera past (all silent they,
   Too fresh their grief for intermit of word),
Above the trampling of the funeral way
    A sound of mournful music might be heard,
    As if remorse for silence just then stirr'd
The monotone of sorrow. So it is:
   Even too long sorrowful silence seems absurd;
The heart must speak. And better suffer this
Than the melodious moan of melancholy miss,

And also lose the pure heart-moving tale,
   The poet's minor song, that plaint most sweet
Which from the full jug of the nightingale———
    But such reflections vainly now intreat,
    Albeit for our sad subject not unmeet.
Speaking of music,—as I speak there comes
   A clearer sound; and now my sense complete,
As one at feasts discriminates the crumbs,
Mine ear distinguishes the bray of kettledrums.

Broad-headed, prominent-eyed, and shortly limb'd,
   Straight wings diaphonous now undisplay'd

The Kettledrummers pacing slowly hymn'd,   46
In kettledrummish language be it said,   _C.A._ 18
  The laud of that great Cat so grandly laid
Beneath his catafalque, for whom they sang
  (Or instrumented—are not throats too made?)
Their high Magnificat, with mile-heard bang.
Deafen'd I was as near arrived the tuneful gang.

When these had pass'd, ere yet the hymn' was hid
  In the dim distance, came the Grylli by,   47
Crying capriciously "This Cat, he did,
  He did, he did," with iterative cry,
As at an Irish wake—why did he die?
And following their untuned, unvarying din
  Cymbals and Tabors echoed swift reply,   48
The while the Players on the Violins   49
Their bow-legs plied,—one tired, the other leg
                              begins.   _C.A._ 19
All leaping as they went; and in their train
  The Meadow-Dancers, dancing as in Ind   50

_C.A._ 18 "These drums are formed of convex pieces of parchment,
gathered into numerous fine plaits, lodged in cavities on the side
of the body, behind the thorax.   They are not play'd upon with
sticks; but by muscles and cords fastened to the insides of the
drums . . . which enables them to emit an excessively loud sound,
which may be heard at the distance of a mile." _Harris, on
Insects &c. page_ 204.

_C.A._ 19 "The males have not the cymbals and tabors of the
crickets and grasshoppers; their instruments may rather be likened
to violins, their hind legs being the bows. . . . When one be-
gins to play he bends the shank of one hind leg beneath the thigh,
where it is lodged in a furrow designed to receive it, and then
draws the leg briskly up and down. . . . He does not play both
fiddles together, but plays them alternately." _Harris, on
Insects &c. page_ 165.

Those dervishes whom fraud or pious pain
   Compels; and then a sound of rushing wind
Fill'd all the space, and hearers' ears were dinn'd
As swept the locusts by in hot desire,
   Like noise of chariots yet by war unthinn'd
With many horses charging in their ire,
Or crackling of the prairie overrun with fire.

These broke the long procession's equal line:
   Soon link'd up by the Scarabæian guards,—
Each one with vizor closed, as sorrowing sign
   Respectful for the Dead. All eyes towards
   Their glorious panoplies with keen regards
Were cast, some bright with cataphracted gold,
   Some fairly striped and beautiful as pards,
Others in splendid colours manifold,
Catadioptrical, most lovely to behold.

Muse! name a few before they quit thy sight!
   Proclaim their blazons so the world may know
How Robyn honour'd was for all the spite
   Of Fate, too frequent worker of his woe!—
   The shining Areods led in the show,   51
With golden helmet, lemon-colour'd cloak,
   And breeches brown but with a brassy glow,
Shaded with green. No Morning ever woke
More radiantly attired; each bore a sprig of oak.

The spotted Pelidnotæ, plainer dress'd,   52
   Be noted next! with mantle dully red
Spotted with black, and darker bronzèd vest,
   Their nether limbs in bronze green garmented.

With a broad vine-leaf shadow'd each his head.
The Omalophians mark! in chestnut gown.   53
    But look again! The chestnut-colour fled,
'Tis red, 'tis green that overcomes the brown;
And now it takes all hues to Iris' self beknown.

In creamy white, with train of blue, array'd,
    The Melolonthans carry each a rose,   54
A damask rose-bud on a vine-leaf laid.
    Lo where behind them black Atrata goes! 55
    Indian Cetonia follows: as he throws   56
His overcoat of brownish yellow back
    (Sprent with black spots irregular) it glows
With pearly tints. His undercoat is black;
His pantaloons are red. No glory doth he lack.

Humming a tune, he nibbles at a peach,
    Which scarcely tasted he will fling aside:
A reckless rout of ruffians, all and each,
    Cetonia leads. With him his brother, wide 57
Across the chest, and strong, with martial stride;
His armour coppery-lustrous, purplish black:
    One knows him better by his scented hide,
Like Russian leather. Well-betray'd his track!
He hopes not for escape unless pursuit be slack.

See where the giant-born Lucanians stalk!   58
    The after dwarfs will the Snout-bearers be; 59
These Pea-Devourers, stealthy in their walk; 60
    Red tails foretell the Attelabidæ;   61
    Corn weevils these Curculionidæ,—   62
Garb of deep brown cream-spotted they affect.

In violet tinged with green Cerambix see!   63
With velvet black and gold is Clytus deck'd : 64
The golden zigzag bands adown his sides deflect.

As at some noble's funeral may come
  After patrician carriages the shay
Or commoner waggon, so behind this scum
  Of pride in its magnificent array
  The dregs of mourning follow'd : not that they
By me are deem'd unfitted to a Muse ;
  But that time fails me at this turn to say
All their distinctions. Yet a few I choose :
The true historian knows no insignificant news.

The whole tribe of Aphididæ was there,—
  Saltatory Psyllæ and the Aphides :
The last a crowd innumerable,—no pair
  Of eyes could separate such swarms as these,
  Nor quickest thought their differences seize.
The Coccidæ apart were from the rest.
  Little in any was the eye to please :
Some in some kind of tawdry finery dress'd.
Some shabby, taken in mass a lousy lot at best.

Hopp'd next the Tettigonians ; and then came 65
  The sad Corei : well might all be sad,   66
These and the hosts forerunning, for the same
  Knew of the potent enemies they had
  In honest birds, in humane service glad
To rid the earth of predatory kind,—
White-wing'd Lygæons and such robbers bad,   67
  Who with the Phytocorians came behind.   68

Many are there the like, who throng into my mind.

I would go on, and tell you yet of more
　　Who interest took in that dear Cat deceased,
Dreading bird-enmity: ay ! count the score
　　Of trespass, nor omit the very least,—
　　Since Curiosity, insatiate beast !
Asks nothing less of me : but I am tired,
　　And Pegasus demands to be released.
He 'll budge no farther for cat's sake, tho' hired,
Well-fed and ridden well and never more admired.

I could go on.　Do not I hear the wings ?
They crowd upon my gaze ! my poor brains whirl !
The Urocèrids, with spear-headed stings,　　　　69
Harpies that at our feasts their canvas furl,　　70
　　And Tortrices—My note-book's leaves upcurl
As they———
　　　　　　At this the wondrous vision fled.
　I heard Ma talking with a neighbour's girl.
" It is that insect Harris book," Ma said,
" The nasty insect book put maggots in her head."

A Harpy　　　　　　　　　　＼

FUNEREAL CATALOGUE

THE PERSONAGES OF THE PAST PROCESSION.

LEPIDOPTERA

1 Arctia Virgo, 2 Arctia Scribonia, 3 Arctia Virginica, 4 Arctia Urticae or Erminia, 5 Arctia Acraea, 6 Attacus Polyphemus, 7 Ceratocampa regalis, 8 Attacus Cecropia, 9 Liparidae, 10 Lophocampa tesselaris, 11 Aegeriadae, 12 Clisiocampa silvatica, 13 Mamestra picta, 14 Velleda, 15 Geometra, 16 Eudamus Tityrus, 17 Asclepias Syriaca 18 Noctuae, 19 Gortyna Zeae, 20 Clisiocampa Americana 21 Agrotis Devastator, 22 Notodontadae, 23 Pygaera ministra, 24 Eudryas or Bombyx grata, 25 Noctua cubicularis, 26 Saturnia Maia, 27 Nymphalis Ephestion, 28 Trochilium exitiosum, 29 Lophocampa Caryae, 30 Dryocampa senatoria, 31 Papilio Asterias, 32 Pontia oleracea, 33 Sphynx quinquemaculatus, 34 Ceratomia quadricornis 35 Vanessa Antiopa, 36 Choerocampa Pampinatrix, 37 Philampelus Achemon, 38 Arctia Isabella, 39 Hyphantria textor, 40 Attacus Luna, 41 Anisopterix, 42 Saturnia Io, 43 Xyleutes Robiniae, 44 Perophera Melsheimerii, 45 Limacodes pithecium.

HEMIPTERA

46 Cicadae (Harvest-Flies, misnamed Locusts).

Orthoptera

47 Platyphillum concavum, 48 Achetadae (Crickets) and Gryllidae (Grasshoppers), 50 Orchelimum vulgare.

COLEOPTERA

51 Arcoda lanigera, 52 Pelidnota punctata, 53 Omalophia sericea, 54 Melolontha subspinosa, 55 Melolontha atrata, 56 Cetonia Inda, 57 Osmoderma scaber, 58 Lucanidae, 59 Rhyncophoridae, 60 Bruchidae, 61 Atelabus analis, 62 Curculio Pales, 63 Callidium violaceum, 64 Clytus speciosus or Hayii.

HEMIPTERA

65 Tettigoniae, 66 Coreus tristis, 67 Lygaeus leucopterus 68 Phytocoris lineolaris.

HYMENOPTERA

69 Uroceris albicornis.

DIPTERA

70 Musca Harpyia or domestica.

If this tale miscarries,
The fault 's in that HARRIS !
The more curious
     May look
     In his book
For private circulation
" *Of the Insects injurious,*
    To vegetation."
Boston U.S.A., 1862.

King Ceratocampa

THANKSGIVING DAY.

Every day 's no Yule : cast the cat a castock. *Proverb.*
To go like a cat on a hot bake-stone. *Id.*

THANKSGIVING DAY is once a year :
Thanksgiving cheer——Ah, well-away !

Forgive a rhyme like broken sherds !
For length of words grief hath not time.

Sad, sad my tale ; my tears drop hot :
Vain tears, God wot ! they nought avail.

Yet, when I think of happier days,
And all the ways that did so link

My life to his, the tears must fall.
Bliss to recall is bale, I wis.

I see him still, his eyes on mine,
Through woeful brine my eyes full fill.

Again he stands and curls beside,
To have his hide smooth'd by my hands.

That sleek soft fur,—I see it now,
And hear his low contented purr.

I see his stripes of gold and black,
The well-arch'd back, the nose he wipes

With cleanly paw, and that spry taile
(Might bear a flaile—upright as Law),

His shapely legs, stretch'd tow'rd the fire
When hot desire for solace begs,

His comely head hid 'neath his thighs
When coil'd he lies upgathered

A blessed heap snug on my lap—
Asleep mayhap or feigning sleep,

His eyes that blink in light of day
And seem to say " I think I think,"

His gentle claws which hurt not much,
The tender touch of his sheathed paws,

His pretty ways, his clever tricks :
Here, Memory ! fix thy foolish gaze !

Again he climbs my shoulder's height—
His old delight——O happy times !

No more, no more can ye return ———
Fire! wherefore burn? O oven door!

O sad cook wench! Her fingers ply
The dough, for pie, while on a bench

Beside her lies Kok Robyn, who
Hath nought to do but wink his eyes

And watch her work. Alas! who knows
What direful woes in the future lurk?

Now in the dish plump chickens laid,
The white paste made quite to her wish,

She places it on the oven shelf
And turns herself for another fit.

Dear Robyn owns one weak defeat:
He loves the meat on chicken bones.

Her head is turn'd; he enters, sly,—
Behind the pie lies undiscern'd.

Now punkin pies in turn are made,
And, unaffray'd by prophecies,

The making o'er, the pies are slid
Where Robyn 's hid, she slams the door,

Heaps on the coal, the oven heats;
Kok Robyn sweats: Saints save his soul!

F

Muse, draw thy veil ; no mews we heard,
Deaf as a Kurd, she miss'd his taile.

But when the oven yawn'd to yield its freight
Of culinary gifts, what squall was that
Scaring the guests whose hunger had to wait?
The astonied Cook drew out in scatter'd state
Some piecrusts, chicken bones, and one
                              DEAD CAT.

---

* * Our dear Hattie in her fond appeal for the soul of Robyn
had no thought, we are sure, of speaking in any way profanely.
Allowance may be made for the unpreparedness of the sudden
horrific catastrophe.   And she had probably read the writings
of that eminent divine and scholar, Mr. Jno. Skelton, rector of
Dis and poet-laureat to his late excellent Majesty Henry VIII,
in whose erudite poem of "Phyllip Sparowe" we may read—
    "Good Lord, have mercy upon my Sparowe's soul ! "
Also the Rev. Mr. Sterne appears of the same thought, as—
    "A Cat has a soul, an't please your Honour."
Which is more to the purpose.   Absolute originality we do not
claim for Miss Brown, and she should be judged accordingly.

                              EDITOR.

MYSTERY

What a caterwauling you do keep. Shakspere.

WE KNEW on what a thread hung Robyn's life,
And pray'd him to be careful ; but as rife
As ever were his wanderings in and out.
We seldom learn'd ought of his whereabout.
Still, when a week had gone without a sight
Of his fool's tabard, anxious love grew white
With apprehension, troublesome for news.
I did not mention that all kinds of stews
And broils and pies and funeral baked meats,
Even cold, he hated now ; and made retreats
From coals and cinders out into the snow,
Which was quite deep, and never let us know
How to provide for him, so had to fast
For days and days, his mind his sole repast.

The bitter winter had begun at last,
With fitful gusts of wind and stinging snow ;
Then clearer weather, and the earth below
Ice-bound ; and then a poor essay at glow
And possibly a chance of some o' rain ;
Then the white feathers flutter'd down again ;

F 2

Then lace and sparkling jewels hung on the trees,
Next morning booted to their very knees
In white, the delicate slim birches bow'd
Before the majesty of frost, or cow'd
By the mere weight of ice, like milkmaid's yoke;
And under eaves of snow brown walls of oak;
White copings on the hemlocks, and, still seen,
Some slurs of yellow ice beneath the green;
And then again a heavier fall o'erspreads
The landscape, only here and there the heads
Of greyish hedgehog spines above the white,
Those dimly visible.

                 On such a night
Robyn, who since Thanksgiving Day had shirk'd
The warm fire-side, and but too often lurk'd
Where ovens were not, took it in his head,
Or it might suit my taile (he had been fed
On milk scarce thaw'd, within it parboil'd bread)
To wander woodward in this snowy depth o'
Winter, where his wilful vow like Jephtha
Brought him to trouble.   Several mornings kiss'd
The eaves' long icicles; and still we miss'd
Our household Robyn.   Why should I persist
As if I hoped the rime would raise a ghost?
Our Robyn came not: Robyn must be lost.

My uncle Slate (some people call him Slade),
His name was Ebenezer, was by trade
A spirit-dealer.   I don't mean he sold
Spirituous liquors, either hot or cold,
But he call'd spirits from the vasty deep
Glendower-like wholesale, retailing cheap

To whoso would. He was what the poor Injine
Would call a most almighty Medicine,
No medium man. He 'd taken his degree
At Philadelphia or in Germany,
And studied much among the Chippewas,
Where Catlin found him, balancing of straws
And swallowing knives, or acting other sleights
To keep poor ignorant squaws awake o' nights
With admiration of the marvelous man.
By birth he was a full-blood African,
Born at Congo; had join'd a caravan
In youth and visited Egypt, where he learn'd
Mosaic work; had been in the Bush, and burn'd
His skin in Australasian lands; in Ind
Had sometime raised the Devil if not the wind;
Could beat Aladdin's Uncle at his tricks
Of lamps and air-castles; knew how to fix
A ghost by simple twirling of his thumbs;
Had been down Babylonish catacombs
And read on Solomon's Seal the mystic words
That taught him languages of beasts and birds
And fishes, which the same at his command,
A nod, obey'd him; he could understand
Signs of the times, and of the Zodiac;
He had stood with the Devil, back to back,
And faced the whirlwind; he one night had hid
Himself in the middle of the Pyramid
Of Djizeh and conversed with Pharaoh's ghost;
And he had been in Lapland, where they boast
Their Wizards. Even there he ruled the roast.

This was my Uncle, on my Mother's side :

My Father's name was Brown, but fair his hide.
No ebon he, Sir! he was baptised James,
And set no store upon those magic games.
But Mother had of sorcery a spice.
So, when Rob was not found, we sought advice
Of Uncle Eben. Did I say before
He was likewise a joiner, therefore more
Knowing than most folk to put this and that
Together. We would tell him of the Cat
Miss'd so mysteriously, and claim his help
For Rob's recovery. Why, many a whelp
Straying from doting mistress Uncle had
Restored, and oft housewifely hearts made glad
With home-returning spoons or other such:
Wherefore we thought it not presuming much
To use his office for inquiry now,
Difficulty unseen, or I avow
I had not put the old man to such cost.

. He welcomed Ma and me, ask'd what we'd lost,
Knowing, it seem'd, even before we spoke
The purport of our coming; made a joke
Of our anxiety; said all was right,
And he would turn informer that same night;
Kept us to dinner; made us stay to tea;
No one was present there except us three;
And after lights brought in began his mystery.

And first he took a thread that from the shears
Of Atropos was stolen, and round his ears
Bound it 'gainst hearing more than for his good;
And then of the True Cross a splint of wood

He screw'd upon the handle of a flail
From Boaz' threshing-floor,—he said a nail
Would loosen all the charm ; three equal hairs
Of a blue hippopotamus, with cares
Abundant got what time conjunctive Mars
Kiss'd Venus (there 's an influence in stars
Rightly discern'd, and at lunàtic full
A luminousness unseen when days are dull),
These tied he ; and a caterpillar's cocoon
Unwound in water'd whiskey with a spoon
And built of it with care and cunning sleight
The form by children a cat's-cradle hight.
All these on a turn-table he display'd
In fitting order; then in the dark convey'd
A short stump of slate pencil, which he laid
Reverently in the cradle.   Right below
There was a drawer, a slate in it, you know.
Then he began to conjure.   I relate
Only the truth.   Upon the drawer-hid slate
(We all examined it) no sort of sign
Of drawing or of lettering, not a line
Or scratch appear'd as Uncle placed it there.
He bow'd his head as if in earnest prayer
The while we two held hands and shut our eyes.
Then the drawer open'd to our great surprize
All of itself and, as on its own feat, rose
The slate and walk'd upon the table ;   There
Who look'd at it might see a line, all red,—
SEEK THE THREE CATS !—No more !
   Slate scratch'd his head,
And said—"The Three Cats, who the deuce
   are they ? "

But the deuce help'd not : he must have a trey.
He rang the bell ; a tray was brought ; he laid
The slate upon it ; then, as much afraid,
Stood trembling, knee and elbow, he did shake,
And rose his hair.   Ma said—For deary sake,
Don't go no further, Eben dear !   He look'd :
" I raise my Ebenezer here or cook'd   *C.A.* 20
Shall be my goose."   Stiff silence follow'd that.
Methought I heard the mewing of a Cat.
Then categorically voices came :—
" Who are you?   Not to you !   By nether flame !
" I shan't mind you.   Your flames be d—d !—
                                 " You shall
" Answer me !   No, we shan't."—An interval,
And on the tray my Uncle sat him down
Mewing cat-like, and swore, and with a frown
Tore handfuls of his beard, it was quite grey.
" By gosh and Cokys wounds I 'll have my way."
Loudly he raged, and stamp'd ; and then I saw
Come from the dimness a great grey cat's paw,
A claw, and tear my Uncle's barèd arm.
I saw the blood run down and trickle warm ;
It fell into and fill'd the tray.   Then he—
" Only a maid can in this mirror see,
One made of mixèd blood.   Mule Hattie ! you
                                 are She."
Obedient, I look'd down : but looking so,
All whirl'd around, upside downside did go.

C.A. 20 EBENEZER : no pun upon my Uncle's name : the name,
from the Hebrew, signifying Stone of Help, a conjuring place.
I *Samuel*, 7, 12.   See likewise Smith's *Dictionary*.

The level floor on which the tray was put
Stood wall-like. Then in fear my eyes I shut.
"Look forth and see and hear and understand!"
Such is my Uncle's brief and stern command.
I tear mine eyes from blindness, from my ears
Drive out their deafness, cast away my fears,
And with my understanding firmly based
Look in the magic glass before me placed.

What see I there? Three forms of mighty make.
One with her tail twined round her like a snake,
And crouching with her nose upon the fender,
I knew at once, the Cat o' the Witch of Endor:
Grey, awful, with the shadow of a crown
Across her snow-white whiskers dimly thrown.
The second was a swift-limb'd delicate thing
The poet, Shelley, might have loved to sing,
A pard-like spirit, soft, ethereal, slim:
Methought at first that Cat belong'd to him,
But poet intuition may not err,—
I knew the Witch of Atlas honour'd her.
The third, more homely, with a travel'd air,
And black and white, or particolour'd hair,
I had not noticed but for Uncle, cried he—
"You'll need that one for all she learnt o' Friday."
He said no more; it was enough, I knew so
I had to do with the Cat of Robinson Crusoe.

While pass'd such thoughts and introduction gave,
I saw the Three preluding for a stave,
And pacing with a flourish of broomsticks round
A cauldron by three legs held off the ground.

I saw, and listen'd for their voices' sound.

But first from each issued a gentle mew,
As saying—To our old misses and our new
We are sure servants, catechumens true,
Awaiting but the question.
                                    That they knew.
And Uncle told me not a word to speak:
'Twould break the charm or leave it all too weak
   To answer.   Then again a mew, a squeal
In concert, and forthwith on toe and heel
The Cats spun round and round the magic pot
(A fire was underneath to keep it hot),
Each in her offering flinging
And, so obliging, singing
                                    Of what was what.

CAT OF ENDOR

Neck of slain sheep, chop by chop
In the steaming cauldron flop;
Sprinkle well with fresh spring peas;
Drop in then by twos and threes
Delicatest sorts of beans;
Add the smallest hearts of greens,
Cauliflowers, and turnips two,—
Not too big of each will do;
New potatoes without stint;
Early carrots; just a hint
Of lettuce: let us bury these
In fresh lots of tender peas!—
All—Double, double, don't spare trouble!
Let the gravy boil and bubble!

Stir it as a stirrer would!
Serve the mixture hot and good!

CAT OF ATLAS

Throw in raisins by the pound;
Wheat-flour, very finely ground;
Citron-slices, candied o'er;
Currants an abundant store;
Add of brandy just a gill;
Almonds, nutmeg, as you will!
All—Hubble, bubble, boil and bubble!
Don't spare toil, but make it double!
Stir, keep stirring as you would
If the stirring did you good!

CAT OF CRUSOE

Drop in sugar, sugar—mind!
Rubb'd on juicy lemon-rind;
Melt it with a little rum;
Pour in tea to overcome
Spirit influence; then add
Brandy enough to make you glad;
Next of lemon slices slim,—
They are just right if they swim;
Fill with rum up to the brim!
All—Let it not quite boil or bubble;
Spare not care, and double trouble;
Stir it as a stirrer should:
Have it hot, and strong as good!

CAT OF ATLAS

And now our He-Cat call!
Grand Master of our rites, approach!

I hear the wheels of his old rumbling coach,
And the steps fall.

                    HE-CAT *appears*

   H.C.—How now, my dears!
My little kittenish frisky frolicsome Cats!
What is 't ye do?

   All—A deed without a name
      I do; and I; and I the same.

   H.C.—And that 's?

   C. of E.—I make a stew.

   C. of A.—I broth.

   H.C.—   And you?

   C. of C.—   I brew.

   H.C.—The name! the name!

   C. of E.—HOTCH-POTCH my stew.

   C. of A.—PLUM-BROTH I do.

   C. of C.—RUM-PUNCH.

   H.C.—   Well, through
With the incantation though it nought avails!
But let me think, first looking at my nails :—
It must, it must be so.—Tie your three tails
Together; part knot suddenly; and sing,
Dancing about the great Pan in a ring,
      To the Egyptian Sphynx,
      True Cat, if ever one!—
      My task is done.
      Kiss me and let me go!
      Good! good! good!—so
        Each minx,
    Good-b'ye! farewell, fair Three!
      My spirit Pussy see
Sits on a cat-tail leaf, and mews for me!

And now the trinal links
Are join'd and sunder'd ; nimbly, toe and heel,
The Cats spin round the charmed pot.
And the fire never sinks,
But ever grows more hot
As thus they make appeal

To the Great Sphynx.

O Cat most fair !
Listen where thou art squatting
Amid the yellow hot Egyptian sands
On twisted braids of palm-leaf matting,
The wet ends of thy Nile-steep'd dropping hair
Licking for mere coolness' sake !
Goddess and no mistake !
Hear our demand !
Listen and reply to us !
In the name of gouty Œdipus,
Whom thou wouldst have gobbled down
Had he not thy secret known ;
By all thy conundrum'd ghosts,
Thy unguessts, the riddle-lost ;
By great Memnon's morning song
Murmuring thy ears among,
And Isis' yet remember'd hymn ;
By the desert lion grim,
In safe covert of thy breasts
Seeking shelter when the crests
Of the Simoom him affright ;
By thy shadow in moonlight
Reaching o'er uncounted miles ;

By those Cleopatric smiles ;
By thy necromantic wiles ;
By thy lips oracular ;
By all subtleties, which are
Cat-like ; by thy woman face,
And bosom full of goddess grace ;
By thy never uncoil'd tail ;—
Let our prayers with thee prevail ;
　　Lift, lift thy enigmatic head,
　　With hoar centuries' dust bespread ;
　　Listen and give quick reply !
　　Lay thy ruinous kisses by ;
And thy most headlong rebuss waive
Till thou our question answer'd have
　　　　Of this Cat's grave !

Singing the Cats spun with swift wheel
Around the pot, more swift than winks
　　　　Or looks of lynx,
　　　Repeating their appeal.
　　　I listen'd, most afear'd.
　　　What next ? methinks.
　　What wonder next appear'd ?

　　　Uprose the Sphynx
On her hind legs tremendous ; laid one paw
Upon her stony lips, as in deep thought,
　　　　Then hollowly brought
This answer forth, from that capacious maw
　　　Which ne'er before
　Since Lord Osiris built her in the sand
　　　Obey'd command.

Where o'er
  A cat-like fruit while purple flowerets wave
Look for his grave!
                    I heard, I saw no more,
Nor knew till Uncle bow'd us to the door.
Not wiser, but some sadder for our trip,
We went our ways; still hidden in my brain
          Those Sphynx words did remain,
And to my recollection slowly came again.
I waited the event.

Months pass'd.   The icy grip
Of winter was relax'd ; and icier grief
                    Sprang also to relief.
Spring came and went;
And punkin vines 'gan run
Across our lot, and also, one by one,
Increase of punkin self to bask it in the sun.
I was a-reading Darwin's *Loves of Plants*,
Mother beside me, in my Father's pants
Setting a patch.   Our punkin patch is green.
I thought of the later D, what did he mean
By his developments.   Am I a dunce?
Were cats and serpents vegetables once?
I know some plants are climbers, others crawl.
Does that the animal destiny forestall?
A sort of archetypal hint of what
May be this Punkin's or that Squash's lot:
Good-sized developing their legs become
Real Cats; the smaller, or the stay-at-home
Can not be more than Serpents or at most
Go Caterpillar-like.   And so I lost,

As older thinkers do, myself in dreams
Of supermundane cosmocomical schemes,
Till looking off, by what but pure good luck?
One of our punkins my attention struck.
It was so like a couchant cat,—indeed
Like Robyn, just of the same motley breed,
With a long stalky tail, but wanting legs.
Headless and round as beer or whiskey kegs.
Alas, his bier! his spirit!   Could it be
He had gone back to punkinninity,
Reverse development?   If forward flies
The grower to accord with novelties,
Might he not also, ceasing thus to yearn
Far forward, take an undeveloping turn?
Why not?   My Robyn, underneath the snow,
Used not his legs, and therefore let them go ;
Could not keep head against the weight of ice,
So the head waited not.   It was not nice
To find him lost so : but I knew he thought
Some punkins of himself.   That solace raught ;
And I examined further, as recurr'd
The oracle, the Sphynx' mysterious word—
" Look for his grave . . white . . purple "
                              so they were!
A plant—arcanic powers! the plant is there
And waving over that same punkin's growth.
Graceful and tall—I 'll take my Bible oath,
Hairy—if I have two eyes in my head,
Ash-colour'd—sure in memory of the Dead,
Long tapering leaves, a very wealth of bloom
Purple and white!   It is my Robyn's tomb!
O'er his dear dust doth the white banner wave.

"Keels rosy and wings red" my Botany gave,
And "T Virginiana." It is he,
My virgin love, my Robyn, F.F.V.   *C.A.* 21
T is Tephrosia—Truly winter froze—   *C.A.* 22
Froze your hot heart, my dear! My taile must
                                        have its close.
Look, Ma! She look'd; then with her fingers groped
   About the punkin's root——and, as I hoped,
   One little bone she uply rummagèd.   *C.A.* 23
   "The last joint of his pretty taile!" she said.
   I saw—the rest was there. Then knew I he was
                                        dead.

C.A. 21 Feline, *i.e.* First Families of Virginia. Myself am Georgian.

C.A. 22 TEPHROSIA VIRGINIANA, Gr. *tephros*, ash-coloured, vulgarly Goat's Rue or Cat-gut : the reason why Robyn's bowels yearned for it as his place of burial. Obnoxious to serpents, says Aristotle.

C.A. 23 The bone LUZ, *Os Coccygis Robinii*, which according to the Rabbins is the only bone to withstand dissolution. On this comes the body at its final resurrection.

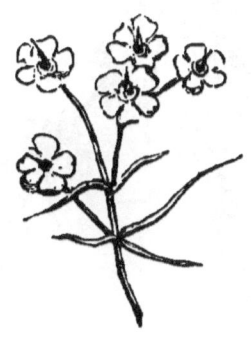

CATASTASIS

At Catalani's song the angels glode
   Earthward to listen : so at Robyn's Feast
My Muse, that somewhat catadoxly rode,
Had power lent back to effort had increased
   The high cat-asterism. Rob's abode
Were now Catabibazon, at the least.

* * CATASTASIS is the climax preceding the conclusion.
CATALANI, in religion S. Cecilia. CATADOXLY, passing
the experiences of other poets or those of my own youth.
CAT-ASTERISM, the Catalogue of Stars. CATABIBAZON,
the place of most starry honour in the south node of the
Great Dragon his taile.

THE SQUASH

HOW THE SQUASH BECAME A CAT

WE HAVE a beautiful cat in our possession, so far
as one can be said to possess a cat (since the days of
witchcraft the title to possession is not quite so clear),
a he-cat of the striped or striated kind, striped like a
very squash. We were lying the other day on our back
in our orchard, staring up into a streaked-apple tree,
and thinking, as the apples fell, of little Isaac Newton
and the curious upcomes after falls. From Newton's
apple tree our thoughts fell off to Darwin, meanwhile
Rob lying on our lap, purring out his heart's content,
and probably thinking in his feline fashion. Near us
was a fence dividing our lot from neighbour Smith's,
and, even as we looked, over this fence a wild squash
was climbing. How often we had tried to keep it on
our own side. Noticing it again, we were puzzled by
the strange likeness between the squash (striped too)
and Rob, particularly as regarded Rob. It struck me
then that both were climbers. Often we had watched
them in sunshine and in moonlight, and day or night
Rob was just as difficult as the squash to keep on the
home side of the fence. Darwin in our thoughts, the
question arose—Why this? What is the cause of the

common instinct? Dogs do not climb fences to their
neighbours' lots; cats and squashes do. What is the
special relationship? There did not seem much to be
made of it; so we returned to the book which before
our mind wandered had been our study, our favourite
Horace Greeley's *What I know about farming*. There
at page 1273 (but not in all the editions) look at this
in a foot-note:—

ON THE INFLUENCE OF SOIL.

"I recommend that the squash be planted in a light, sandy
soil. A streak of green marl is an advantage if you have it.
I have found by repeated sowings that the colour of the fruit
is much handsomer, resembling the beautiful streakiness of
a ripe apple, only that the hues are not so vivid, the flavour
also sometimes not unlike apple-sass. I have been told, but
I do not know this of my own observation, that the peculiar
streakiness of English bacon, so much prized by Cincinnati
importers, is obtained in a similar manner (which is likely),
the pigs from their tenderest infancy being fed in turn upon
red and white potatoes, raised on differently coloured soil. *
It is said too that the alternate layers of fat and lean are got
by feeding one day and starving the next; but this does not
run with my argument, which is only racy of the soil."

Elsewhere he observes:—
"It is known that the striped flag (Iris Americana) common
on this Continent thrives best in mixed clays. And the use
of stripes in cultivation has ever been asserted at the South."

These be practical remarks! The squash's colour is
then, as Mr. Greeley's experience shows, mainly owing
to the soil. Now to look at it Darwinningly. In early

---

* "The same is seen in clovers, the colour depending on the soil, not
without effect on the cattle: after the manner of Jacob with Laban."

youth the squash is green, in old age yellow, in middle
life neither but with an inclination either way. There
must of course be a moment when neither the yellow
nor the green inclination predominates, accident, time,
something or other, gives the predominance. Suppose
opposite accidents, and these frequent and alternating.
Is it too much to perceive that the outer appearance
must express some sign of the inward struggle, and so
a stripe, *of course very faint at first*, is produced? No
question then as to the influence of soil! Other cases
also occur to us in its support. The political stripe in
the District of Columbia is often due altogether to the
soil : green first, and then distinctly marked as yellow,
even statesmen who think themselves " some punkins."
It may be the same with squashes. Mr. Greeley ought
to know. He tells us *the mixed clay fixes the tendency.*
Granting, we say, the influence of soil, then in time—
it may be ages, time is a relative,—in time the stripes
fixed regularly will be permanent. We have the first
step cat-ward. The next step is for climbing. That
squash on the fence seems opening its cat-like eyes in
amazement. It may look far-fetched to talk of eyes,
but if potatoes have eyes and corn ears, why not——
We are rambling, like the squashes. One thing is sure.
In old Indian days,—early, if not the earliest squash
days,—the boundaries of their hunting-grounds and
plantations were not stable; beside which the squash
could hardly be said to be converted from aboriginal
wildness. Even the Mississippi does not heed bounds.
Say that a native chief pulled stakes and took in a bit
of a neighbour's patch, took it in too against the sun ;
your squash, having a habit of growing that way, also

preferring the soil on the old side of the paling, what
does he, no doubt after many vain attempts to wriggle
between the bars, but climb over? Once done is done
for ever. Not even a squash can go back on destiny.
The next generation repeats the climb. In the course
of centuries it becomes habit, helped all through, you
mind, by *the temptation sun-ward*. Still the squash is
but a squash. Wait awhile! From the great English
naturalist, Hood (the elder Thomas, not Jesse), may
be learned how he once furtively buried a male cat of
a sandy-reddish colour under a gooseberry-bush. Up
to that date the berries had been smooth-skinned and
green : *next year they were all hairy and of a red colour.*
They were hairy ever after.* Now only consider this.
If a tiger got buried beneath a wide-spreading squash
tree (the size is no obstacle, for we know that Jonah
sat under a gourd of the same species, and there were
tigers in those parts), the squash next year would be
hairy too, and as much hairier than the gooseberry as
the tiger is larger than the ordinary cat. It is equally
reasonable to believe that if the hair had long influence

---

* We can say something ourselves, even from our own very limited
experience, in confirmation of these freaks of Nature, as they may be
ignorantly called. We ourselves grew a pumpkin over a buried horse.
One pumpkin born on this plant increased to such a bulk that a horse
could go in at one end not stooping and come out with his head down
at the other. And, which was more curious, the seed of this identical
pumpkin was found to be an infallible cure for hoarseness. This was
a Connecticut pumpkin, growth and pedigree both, and on exhibition
in New Haven, when the daily journals made weeks' income in praise
of the occasion. The bearing one thing has upon another, say through
various grafting, is truly marvelous, and should make us pause before
daring to discredit the deeper things of science.

the tiger's claws would not be without. After certain time may be found on the squash a roughness, which on microscopic examination is perceived to be only a *rudimentary claw*. In climbing, that confirmed habit continued, such claws, being useful, become more and more developed. Then as the pendulous squash drops, the heavy body straining from the claws projects some lengthening semblance of limbs; now the winds drag them, the claws hold firm, the heavy body swings, and so the limbs become jointed. Beginning of flexibility only, then, perhaps from sudden wrenches, are breaks, which in mild weather partially recohere and become *articulated joints*. Of course all this is not supposed to be the development of one individual squash. These changes are gradual, the work of centuries, of it may well be eons. We can not observe them now, but we can see suggestive and like indications. It may have taken ages for the development of a claw; how much more for production of a whole limb, joints, the entire and perfect animal. We have nearly reached that in our progressive stages. It may be objected that there is no reason why there should be exactly and only four legs. It must not however be forgotten (Mr. Darwin indeed lays great stress on this) that something is due to original inheritance. There is always the tendency to recur to the primitive type. The primitive type is here tigrine, *as regards the animal development* of what we may still call the Cat-squash. And also many legs might be found to hinder climbing. Notice that it is the cultivated squash to which we have come, that has to climb, not forest trees, *but fences*. Between rail and rail some of many legs would hang useless. Of disuse comes atrophy; the superabundant legs drop off, and the Squash-Cat retains only four as fitting to its latest life. Then only, in the wonderful economy of Nature, as the polliwog becomes the perfect frog by throwing off his tail, the squash perfects the cat with that hereto useless appendage, the old-squash stalk pulled from the parent plant as the new animal departs on adventures, over and off the fence this time, to meet its neighbour and begin the family of house and garden tigers—our familiar Tabby-Cats.

There! our Rob is among the squashes. You may think that he is only a well-developed squash himself, and that still squash basking yonder in the sun really a yet-unanimalised Tom-Cat. "Can such things be and overcome us?" etc.

NOTE by the Editor. This Squash Story is the only prose work of Hattie's which has been preserved; and this in some measure might be esteemed poetry, here only the rough draft (we find the same in Chaucer) designed for future versification.

Since it was written the likelihood of such transformations has been enforced by Professor Newbury, who tells of a Caterpillar, I believe in New Zealand, the larva of which when buried about three inches below the surface, becomes a Vegetable, "retaining the outlines and markings of the parent caterpillar," and growing to a considerable height, having a curious furry ornamental head, caterpillarish. The plant is of a fungoid type, excellent eating, containing much hydroxaethylidentrimethylammonium hydrate, said to be not poisonous, resembling cabbage.

This appears also to favour the retrogressive theory suggested by Miss Brown in her ninth fytte.

THE MEANING OF IT

How many cats' tails to reach the sky? *Old Proverb.*

LIKE to a kettle at a dog's tail, making music as he goes, or may be only musical echoes, so before I close my catalectual budget I propose to say a few words on the Myth. Which may stand as pith of my wandering in Cat-Land, not to be dispensed with. I would have you to understand my writing hath some direction and is not without choice of path. I rejoice also to make correction here and there, as where I spoke of Fiddler Catte as but among my Rob's forbears. In that I did him wrong. Of all forbearing folk he was indeed the head. For there's an ancient rich ante-Arian perhaps myth, with which we have to deal, and ought not any how to miss. The peel of this, no weed, we all of us may read, the well-known rhyme, a screed of earliest time when the world yet was young, and which doubt not was sung amid reechoing spanks, 'neath Himalayan flanks, to children on their nurses' laps, perhaps upon

Euphrates banks ere Babylon was.   This is it, as first
writ in pure Sanscrit, a hymn of the *Rigvedas* :—

HYD ID LDI DLTH'K ATANT HEPHI DLTH KOUJV
MP TA UV URTHMUN CYRNIKH OLALA PHT TUCE
CUT CHSPAU TAN DDYCHRHA NAWAWYT HYS PUN

Of which, according to the best scholars, the English
given almost literally is as follows :—

> The myth is not addled——
> The Cat fiddle-faddled ;
> In the high sky sky-daddled,
> The Cows jump'd over the Moon ;
> The Little Dog (*Cur Nicola*) laught
> At the Moon over-raught ;
> And the dish ran away with the spoon.

The Cat in Hindu mythology is the Moon, the Cow a
cloud.   The moony Cat fiddles, plays like the Cat on
the sign-board : the weather is neither foul-ward nor
fine-ward.   Skydaddled * over the heavens, the white
cow-clouds, perhaps a herd, leap over her.   The moon
so blurred and obscured, twilight seems to return, to
the delight of the "little dog" Canicula, Sirius himself,
the Dog of Twilight, who, not seeing the moon return
from behind the clouds, imagines himself lord of the
situation.   Of one relation the meaning is not so clear.
The Dish may symbolize the round moon-disk, which
that Spoonful of Cow was to carry off, carried instead
as the clouds are lost in the moonshine.   This is only

---

* SKY (not ske) DADDLED, scattered, as aforesaid from the old Irish
Bible, there *sqndad ol*, is plainly identical with Danish *skye dedehl*:
throwing light upon the acquaintance of the Phenician (or yet earlier
Arab) navigators with Ireland, and the Baltic through the Cattegut.

a guess. It may be a hint that the larger can not stint
for the less ; or merely the myth itself running off with
the means that should have raught for us its meaning.
So important leaning excuses so much explanation.

I must acknowledge also to reading that it is not the
home-loving Cat, but the Grasshopper, the Locust, in
the attitude of preyer, which is placed at the top of the
New Troy Exchange. However, on again referring to
the *Rigvedas* I find the Cat frequently indentified with
or rather perhaps connected with the Grasshopper in
the moon myths. In the *PanCat-tantrums* Carabbas
(the soft-sounding C), the Hindu Puss-in-boots, who
lives on Mount Moon, is the Grasshopper, or Leaping
Locust, claiming all he can hop across as his master's.
And he is the original also of our Hop-o'-my-thumb,
whose boots are seven-leagued.

Our own Kok Robyn's first death and burial, or his
burial and first return to life (as we may be pleased to
consider it), is not without a very profound mythical
significance. The Cat on 'Change is a Weathercock.
The Cat and Cock are again identical. It is at night
that the Cat is most active, and it is at moonrise, says
Ælianos, that the Cock exults. So both personify the
moon. And as Sun and Moon through their attributes
are in the old myths interchangeable, so the Cock can
likewise be taken as the Sun, his crest symbolizing the
same, and his names, Cristatus, Cristiger, Cristens, as
the christian poet Prudentius tells us. Our tortoise-
shell Cat, in the Sanscrit Mùshakàràtis, the brindled
mouse-eater, the golden-haired cloud-devourer, whose
hairs are the Sun's rays, takes fitly therefore the name
of KOK ROBYN, the red-breasted twilight in which the

Sun or, as seen in our present version, the Moon rises.
But the SETTER's time comes, the setting ordered by
DAN APOLLO as the Moon disappears at dawn. UNION
is the twilight that unites day and night, hears night's
dying groans, and JACK,* the Sun again, on his back,
not yet fairly risen, only half awake, has his eye upon
him. The Hindu Moon is male. NELLIE (a sisterly
diminutive of Helen—Helios, the Sun) is early-rising
Aurora, who bosses the Moon-funerals. The pall is of
course the heavens. But here seems some confusion,
("a limb o' thee" referring rather to the body) as if
parts of two strophes had been lost and a transcriber
had agglomerated the fragments. TIMOTHY is surely
nothing if not an alias for Thomas the doubter, who
must touch the body to be sure of its death or, in the
legend otherwise applied, who leaves not his bed till
the risen Sun shall kiss his finger-tips. O'DONOGHUE
sounds suspiciously like Don'tknowwho, but the name
is Sanscrit too, or earlier. In the *Pan Cat-tantrums* his
boat is often spoken of, the mystic boat in which the
Sun by night and the Moon by day travel underneath
the ocean; and it may be that as "chief mourner" he
here assumes the office of the modern Charon. So he
may carry the body, and Tim and his fellow denizens
of the air be only wanted as appropriately for the pall.
The Dog, a cat-dog, LEO, who utters K.R.'s Epitaph,
is the dog of Diana, also Sirius, the Star of Twilight.
Whence, from the elder legend (the Moon there being

---

* Here again we have a new form of the Sun Myth : Jack the Giant-
Killer being only Hercules Redivivus, and Heracles himself the Greek
reformed Indras, a very ancient King Arthur or John Brown.

male), we have the Dog with our Man in the Moon.
The rest of the allegory (cloud-mice etc.) is plain.

A very similar myth may be observed in the FIGHT
WITH THE DOG : the contest between Day and Night,
or Light and Darkness, under new forms assigned to
them : the Dog "half blood-hound and half bull," the
Cat brindled as a moon-calf. The THIRD FYTTE has
yet another aspect. Here it is the strife between the
golden haired Apollo and the white Moon-cat. The
Moon takes possession of the black cat—Night ; and
in the FOURTH FYTTE the dejected Sun-god descends
seaward. In the FIFTH his butter-ears reappear. No
need to track the myth throughout. The cord round
Rob's neck (SIXTH) is symbolical of the Sun again,
(the robin is sacred to S. Martin); and the SEVENTH
and EIGHTH are fit joints of the taile of Lamentations
for Thammuz—Thomas Cat—Adonais—Adonis—the
Sun or Moon.

Thus may we interpret the Myth of the Cat-Moon,
so much of it as need be tied to our own tailes. The
myth meaning the Sun would have the Cock as hero,
instead of the Cat. NELLIE then will be the evening
splendour which undertakes his setting, and the other
persons of the drama change characters accordingly.
In the *Taithriya-brahmanum* the crimson-vested bird
of dawn, the Lark (Bharadvâgas) sings, as the Robin,
all day through to the many-coloured birds, but gives
his heart to the little dusky Wren (Iyattikâ-çakuntikâ),
the brown dusk Eventide. For this the Sparrowhawk
relentlessly pursues him with his hate, and eventually
kills him. All the birds who had loved him assemble
to his funeral. The promised wine, his loving pledge

to Jenny, their bridal sacrament, is his own life-blood.
The dusk brown evening boasts its ruddy heaven, yet
ruddier than the early morning glow as Robin's blood
is of a richer tint than all the glory of his living coat.

It is the ever-changing solar song.
Is it not too the universal tale,
The pancattantrums of all-changing Love?
When crimson-clad Cophetua from his throne
Wooeth the Nut-brown Maid, 'tis burly Rob
And homely Jennie in a new disguise.
Call it also, to point some moral here,
The Glory on the lap of Evening Calm,
The bright serenity of a well-spent life.
So every thing aye meaneth some thing else.
Eheu, Jehu! As the Wise Cat observed
To the Philologist—" Man everywhere
And at all times is man." Here ends my taile.

If any ask—Why this or that forget?
Let it to a Cat's short memory be set!

L'ENVOI

GO, LITTLE BOOK!
Who on you look,
Who read you fair,
Will own the young
With thewes unstrung
Not vainly sung
Nor need despair.
This did I write
For Self's delight;
Who list may read:
I have no greed
For pay or praise.
My little Book,
Done all alone,
Fame shall thee own
Past many days.
Go thou thy ways,
Unheeding fleas—
Skip-critics: these
Make no heart ache.
ART FOR ART'S SAKE
Is all my geste:
Some high behest
Let others take!
For me Art is enough,
According to the canon

Of later days (quant : suff :).
And who shall lay a ban on
Me?   My will's my pleasure :
I admit no moral master ;
And so I keep the measure,
Slower in time or faster,
My feet clear from disaster,
I care not whom I offend.
God send my readers good digestion !
That's not the question :
I have not been ordain'd
As preacher ; in no wise
Am given to sermonize ;
My text trots self-explain'd.
Enough if with some art
I play the Jester's part,
With cap and bells to please
Lord Idlesse, and dry peas
All pleasantly perverse
To rattle in his ear.
Yet do I not rehearse,
In strains his soul to move,
Fierce War and faithful Love,
And Truth not too severe
But fashionably dress'd,
Pale Grief and pleasing Fear,
And other tyrants, Robyn ! of the breast ?
What matters whom I choose
For hero?   Must my Muse
Tread heels of Alexander,
Of Walker, of Pizarro,
Napoleon, or Suwarow,

Or other Greek or Roman
Or French heroic gander,
Or common or uncommon?
Why is not Philip Sparrow
As good as Philip's Son?
And what has Homer done
That he may sport his mice,
Frogs and such vermin nice,
And I not own a Cat?
By Helicon, and that
Is a fair poet's oath,
Your frogs and mice are, both,
No fitter for bards' words
Than is my Cat: my sherds
Of rhyme, lame verse at best,
And other faults confess'd,
Of catachresic sort
Et cetera. Though short
To wear the Homeric weed,
Mere catagraphs indeed
And catalectic they,
As modest Frenchmen say;
Albeit catenate,
Which is but fair to state;
Yet, by Apollo's shell,
Of tortoise too, so well
By that mercurial child
Fashion'd when he defiled
Sol wroth for loss of beef,
By him of poets chief,
And by the Muses nine,
I swear these mews of mine

H

Shall win the world's belief.
While Cats are light o' love,
Or Caterpillars move
Cat-like toward their prey,
While every dog his day
Must have, and cats delight
In vows of Catti knight,
So long as at the fire
Cats toast their tailes, till ire
Of cat and dog down dwindles,
So long shall my poor spindle's
  Yarn provoke applause.
  Ay! and by Cokys jaws
  And his nine-jointed taile,
Eyes, heart, by Rob's each wail
And permanent purring note,
  By his one motley coat,
  Yea! by its every hair,
  Black, white, red, gold, I swear
These wakes of him shall live
A nine-fold life, nor sieve
Of Fame refuse them through.
And reasons are there too
Why even a Critic's gall
Should spare my song. I'm small
  And young, a little girl;
  And now first tempt the whirl-
Pool of professional ink.
In truth, upon the brink
I did a little loiter
With modest maiden's coy
  Tergiversating dread.

But then meheard it said,
" Tis a true Muse invites,
And while the maggot bites
Adventure!" Was I wrong?
Came else uncall'd my Song.
Well, words I wrote are writ:
Poor caterings, I admit:
As such do I present 'em.

ADDITAMENTUM

GO, LITTLE BOOK! from Author's solitude :
I cast thee on the market : go thy ways !
And if (so Southey) not too vainly good,
The world may own thee after many days.
When Holland 's read, and Miller kinder view'd,
Poor Hattie Brown may hold her hat for praise.
Would L. C. M. pronounce my verses fine,
I 'd own I think a many worse than mine.

Or, borrowing good words of Mr. Thos. Watson :

" My littel Booke ! goe hie thee hence awaie,
Whose price (God knowes) will countervayle no part
Of pains I tooke to make thee what thou art :
And yet I joie thy birth."

And of Master Hawes in his *Pastime of Pleasure* :

" Go, little Book ! I pray good hap thee save
From miss-metring by wrong impression ;
And who that ever list thee for to have,
That he perceive well thine intention."

As likewise the worthiest Mr. Geoffrey Chaucer:

" And for there is so great diversitie
   In Englishe and in wryting of our tongue,
   So pray I God that none miswryteth thee,
   Ne thee mismetre for default of tongue ;
   And redde wherso thou be, or elles sung,
   That thou be understood God I beseeche."

Thus have I fingered the basket, beheld the holy
barley (is it but hurly-burly?), fed on the drum-
head, and drunken of the liquor of satisfaction.
O Orpheus, thou wildcat charmer! have I not at
this thy feast said *Konz omtoz*, and it is finished !

FINIS CORONAT
(Is my work one to groan at?)
O PUSS !